THE FINN'S TALE

MIKE HORWOOD

 Ward Wood Publishing
www.wardwoodpublishing.co.uk

Published by Ward Wood Publishing
6 The Drive
Golders Green
London NW11 9SR
www.wardwoodpublishing.co.uk

The right of Mike Horwood to be identified as the author of
this work has been asserted by him in accordance with the
Copyright, Designs and Patent Act, 1988.
© Mike Horwood 2011.

ISBN 978-0-9566602-7-5

Designed and typeset in Garamond by Ward Wood Publishing.
Cover design by Mike Fortune-Wood
Cover image © Mad Geek
Title "Girl Picking Mushrooms in Forest"
Agency Dreamstime

Printed and bound in Great Britain by
Imprint Digital, Seychelles Farm,
Upton Pyne, Exeter, Devon EX5 5HY

THE FINN'S TALE

For Eevi, who told me her own Finn's tale

Author's Note

The use of both American English and British English vocabulary and grammar is intentional.

Chapter One

Right from the start, Finland surprised me. When I arrived in Helsinki the temperature was 80 degrees Fahrenheit and it was one of the warmest places in Europe. For that day, at least. It didn't stay that way the whole summer. Coming out of Helsinki airport the heat was noticeable and I felt overdressed in a sweater and jacket. I'll admit to having been thrown a little off balance right at the beginning of my Finnish experience. I had always thought of myself as partly Finnish, which I am; my grandparents on my father's side emigrated from Finland to America in 1920. And although, at the age of forty-four, this was my first-ever visit, I'd always thought of Finnishness as something I could take for granted in my idea of myself. And now here I was, being caught out by the weather, just like all the other tourists. It's true, though, that Finnishness had played a negligible part in my upbringing. In a way, it had been conspicuous by its absence, but that absence was always present, if you take my meaning. I felt it was there as a kind of backdrop against which all the immediate experiences of everyday life took place.

Childhood memories of my grandparents are rather limited. My grandfather died when I was eleven. My grandmother lived a further five years, but for some of that time she was in a nursing home. I visited her only a few times with my parents and I don't have happy memories of those visits. She must have deteriorated into dementia pretty quickly. I can't remember any conversation that I had with her in that nursing home and very likely our communication would have been a bare greeting on arrival and a departing farewell. She has remained quite clearly in my memory as a frail, shrunken figure in a wheelchair, with a tartan blanket round her legs and a shawl round her shoulders, or a small head above the sheet and blanket of her bed, with wispy, silver hair and a frightened look in her eyes. I don't think I registered the fear at the time but it's clearly there in my memory of her at the end. Fear of dying, or fear due to not comprehending who the people around her were or what was happening. Right at the end, she lost her command of English and reverted to Finnish, which cut her off from her surroundings even more. I have wondered whether she believed that she was still in Finland then, virtually the whole of her adult life erased, and that in her mind she was in the farmhouse where she had grown up.

My memories from earlier days, when my grandfather was still alive, are much more pleasant, but because I was so young a lot has faded. I remember my grandfather telling me stories about Finland when I was still very small: over five, but well under ten. I remember them now as pictures; cutting down trees in a forest, fishing with nets through a hole in the ice, and building a roof on a house. Odd, disconnected events that I'm sure must have been elements in longer stories, but only these details have remained. I also remember, very vividly, my grandmother showing me a map of Finland and pointing out the location of her childhood home. All through my childhood and into adulthood I've always been able to put my finger on the spot on the map, with reasonable accuracy, but I forgot the name of the village until I made a point of finding it out again later in life. I have a clear picture, associated with the map memory, of a field, farm buildings and some figures which I strongly suspect must be derived from a photograph, or perhaps several, that she showed me.

Maybe my grandparents themselves were in some of those photos, taken in their youth. I don't remember now, though. Like most small children, I thought of my

10

grandparents as always having been old, always the way that I knew them.

I didn't speak the Finnish language at all. My grandparents used to speak Finnish together but with me they always used English, which they spoke fluently but with an accent and strange pronunciation of some words. They made mistakes with some irregular verbs, too. They did teach me the names of some things in Finnish, most of which I've forgotten, though sometimes one surfaces in my mind. I've even had the experience, in mid-conversation, of getting the Finnish word for something and not being able to find the English word, as if Finnish had temporarily displaced English, which has made it easy to understand how it happened to my grandmother so completely. A bit embarrassing. It's only happened very rarely, though.

The faint trace of Finnishness that came down to me was entirely due to my grandparents and I realize now, with hindsight and adult understanding, that there must have been some regret, for them, in the backgrounding of my family's Finnish past. I see now that they were trying to instill some small element of Finnishness in me. My father, on the other hand, showed little interest in that part of his history. He's never visited Finland, doesn't speak about the country, expressed no emotion when Finland won the ice hockey world championship in 1995 for the first, and so far only, time. He certainly grew up with a basic knowledge of Finnish but later in his childhood he virtually refused to speak the language. I have no idea whether, or how fluently, he would be able to speak it now and, when I once asked him, he said that he didn't know himself and changed the subject. For a long time I didn't know why my father felt this need to deny, in a way, his Finnish past. I'm still not sure, but in Finland I found out a possible explanation.

Actually, 'deny' is too strong a word. He's never denied, or even tried to conceal, the fact that his parents were born

11

and grew up in Finland. He hasn't changed the family surname, Makinen, to something more anglicized, though that might be because he thought it sounded like a Scottish name anyway.

It's funny that all the Finnish first names in my family either sound almost English or convert very easily. My grandmother was Sylvi, which can be pronounced like an English name if you add an 'a' at the end; my grandfather was Aarne, which got pronounced like 'Arnie', short for Arnold. My father's name is Arto, but he has always been known as Art or Arthur. My mother doesn't have a Finnish background. Her name's Elizabeth, though she's always been called Beth. Then there was my aunt Mari, which was always pronounced the same as Marie and, until I went to Finland, I thought that that was how it should be pronounced. My grandparents' last son was christened Mark, with the English spelling, though it's very similar to the Finnish name, Markku. The next generation all have English names: my sister is called Linda and my brother, James. My name is Leonard, or Len. Len Makinen. There's nothing Finnish-sounding about that.

No, in my father's case, it's more ignoring than denial, what you might term a cultivated disinterest. I've always suspected that he has felt some kind of need to make a choice between that Finnish past, which would have been a much closer and stronger presence to him than to me, and his American present, and that rejecting Finnishness was part of his signaling the strength of his commitment to America. It's as if he had to choose between being a Finn and being an American and he wanted to be the latter. I believe that has been important to him, though I've recently also come to understand that other elements may well have exerted an influence. I think, also, that it accounts for that sense of the absence of Finnishness in my own childhood experiences. I was aware of that history through my grandparents. I was aware of its erasure through my father. But to be aware of erasure is also to be aware of the thing erased, so in a strange way erasure served to emphasize the thing it removed. At least for me. I've talked with Linda and Jim about their sense of our Finnish family background and got the impression that it's virtually non-existent. So for them the erasure did lead to absence. It's complicated.

Very soon after they arrived in the United States, so I've understood, my grandparents made their way to Minnesota because there was work to be found there. I believe they moved around a bit during the early years. I don't know details, but I do know that they were up near the Great Lakes in the early days and spent some time in, or near, Duluth. They moved around, but never out of Minnesota as far as I know, and, by the time my father was getting towards his teens, they were settled in St Paul. My mother and father still live there and so do I with my family.

My father was born in Minnesota in 1922, so the Finnish past of his parents was never directly his own. It would always have been something just out of sight, over the horizon. In his early childhood, my grandparents must surely have been in close and regular contact with the relatives they'd left behind in Finland, but those people and places were never a part of his lived experience. It's only recently that I've come to think about how strange it must have felt, especially for a child, to know that you have grandparents alive in the world that you've never seen. I've never heard my father mention his own grandparents. Then at some stage the grandparents my father had never known died. I never knew any dates but I always knew that their deaths pre-dated my birth in 1956. Gradually, the contact between the family members on different continents must have declined. I was aware, during my childhood, that my grandparents had brothers and sisters still living in Finland

13

and I remember them talking to me about my Finnish cousins. I think they may have shown me a photograph. It gave me a strange feeling, I remember, to hear about these people who were, of course, total strangers and as far removed from my life and concerns as possible, referred to with a term of such close relationship. I saw my American cousins on a weekly basis. They were the people I was closest to after my parents and brother and sister. By contrast, these Finnish relatives seemed unreal. Of course, my Finnish cousins were actually second cousins, once removed, but my grandparents didn't use that kind of terminology.

I vaguely remember that news from Finland was discussed between my parents and grandparents, though it would have meant even less to my mother than to my father. I presume this happened when a letter had been received. I can't say how frequent that contact was in those days. I also remember that there were always one or two Christmas cards from Finland each year. They made an impression, I suppose, partly because Christmas impresses the childish mind so strongly, and partly because of the strange language which made these cards stand out particularly.

When my grandmother died in 1972, there was talk about some Finnish relatives coming to America for the funeral. In the end that didn't happen, largely due to the cost and the distance. I was sixteen by then and I remember the discussion about the practicalities of such a trip quite well. I imagine there had been a similar discussion when my grandfather died, but that one I have no memory of.

Such were my experiences through childhood and the impressions they made on my consciousness. I was quite happy to live with the status quo and went through early adulthood without thinking about the family past any more

14

than my father did. I went to university, got started in a career, got married, started a family. I did all the unremarkable, wonderful things that can make life a joy when they go right. And I have no complaints. Then, as I approached the age of forty, something in me must have changed. I found Finnish images rising in my mind more and more. Things that I hadn't realized I remembered. Sudden memories of my grandparents would come unbidden into my head. I would see pictures connected with the stories they had told me. Those same pictures that I've just mentioned. And now I come to focus on this more, in the process of writing it down, I've just realized that the experience of losing an English word and remembering the Finnish equivalent dates from this time. It never used to happen earlier.

The first influence of these thoughts and feelings was that I began speaking to my own two teenage sons, Nick and Alex, about their Finnish ancestry. I was trying to pass on to them some slight sense of Finnishness, as my grandparents had done with me, I suppose. They knew, of course, that their great-grandparents had emigrated from Finland, but nothing more than that bare fact. I started telling them what I could remember of the stories and images that had remained from my contact with my grandparents. I can still see the uncomprehending looks on their faces. They hadn't a clue why I was bringing up this ancient history all of a sudden and didn't understand anything that I was trying to tell them. And I certainly couldn't blame them. I'd never taken much interest in it myself before that time and I began to understand that this reaction that was taking place in me was somehow connected with aging. The emotions I was feeling, the interest that my family history held and the desire to learn more was, for sure, linked to my time of life. When my sons reached forty, then they might want to know something about the past. And then I got my great idea. I would find out everything I could about our Finnish roots. I would produce a family tree and write a family history. I studied history at university and I'd continued to be interested in it and regularly read books on the subject, so it seemed quite logical that I should research my own history. When my boys came of middle age (I invented that phrase, and I'm rather proud of it), they'd be able to get all the information if they wanted it.

I never did it, though. I set out to do it and I thought I was going to do it, but something else came along that turned out to be more important. And so I'm writing this Finn's tale, instead of my own.

Chapter Two

I began my family research project by talking with my father. In one sense it was the obvious thing to do and in another it was the most pointless, given his attitude to the past. Of course, he remembered much more about his own parents than I did and could give me information about their early days in the States. But he could recall almost nothing of whatever facts and stories they'd told about their life and home in Finland. It was no surprise that he had little to say on that subject. He'd spent most of a lifetime deliberately forgetting it. I don't believe he was obstructive on purpose. He genuinely didn't remember much and he genuinely was not interested. He did know the name of the village where they had both grown up, though, and which I could almost put my finger on, on a map. It was called Kuhmoinen, in central southern Finland.

I asked him if there had been any photographs among his parents' belongings after his mother died, thinking particularly of the dimly-remembered farm scene. He said that there had been but that he'd cleared out 'all that old rubbish'. Those were his exact words, and they are clearly indicative of how he felt. Again, I don't believe he was motivated by any desire to hide or deny the past. It simply held no interest for him whatsoever and I'm sure he never anticipated that I would show any.

There was only one way in which he was able to help me advance in my search, and it turned out to be the most important step I took. He had a couple of names and addresses of Finnish relatives, though he couldn't be sure whether these addresses were still valid. Communication had virtually dried up. The Christmas cards had ceased to be exchanged many years earlier, but the occasional letter arrived, usually to inform of a death. The closest contact had been with my father's cousin, a man named Juho Ahonen. My father told me that his own father had felt an especially close bond with Juho, who was the son of his sister, Mari. My aunt Mari was named for her. The older Mari had been two years younger than my grandfather and her son, Juho, had been born just two years before my grandparents emigrated. My grandparents had always taken a special interest in Juho and when he grew up they were in regular contact. These were probably the letters with news from Finland that I had vaguely remembered from my childhood. My father had the idea that his parents had sent presents to Juho at Christmas when he was a child and may have given him some financial assistance at one stage when he was a young adult, although they were never wealthy people themselves.

After my grandparents died, the correspondence shrank to a trickle, perhaps four or five letters in the last twenty years, my father thought. The last had arrived some years earlier and my father couldn't remember whether he'd answered it or not. Those letters had been written in English by Juho's daughter, Aino, with some bits of Finnish which my father may have understood or guessed at. He wasn't very informative about that side of it. He did say that, as far as he could remember, the letters were written as though Aino was writing on behalf of her father, because of the English I presumed, but that the content seemed to be largely Juho's.

Juho, being a bit older than my father, was now quite an elderly man. My father expected that the next letter would probably contain news of Juho's death and that very possibly that might be the end of all communication between the two branches of the family. It seemed as if I'd got my idea of re-establishing contact just in time. I decided to write to Aino to introduce myself.

At this stage I had to ask myself what my goal was in all this. I subtly sounded out Linda and James on the extent of their interest in our Finnish history but they displayed the same indifference as our father. Apparently, my sudden interest was not an inevitable result of reaching middle age, then. So why had it suddenly become so important to me to go back to my Finnish roots and collect the facts that were missing from my picture of that side of my family? Of course, there was the immediate goal of producing a family tree and history, but was there a further motive impelling me?

The answer was not difficult to find; it was clear to me that I wanted to make contact with the descendants of my grandparents' relatives who had stayed in Finland. My Finnish family. I wanted eventually to see the village where my grandparents had grown up, to see the house they had lived in, if it was still standing, and to walk on the land that my ancestors had worked. I realize now, looking back, that I wanted to know what my life might have been if my grandparents had not left. A rather fantastical notion, which would have required my all-American mother happening to meet and marry my father and settle in Finland with him. But my search was not concerned with practicalities. It was an idea, unarticulated at first, that if I could understand who I would have been as a real Finn, I would understand better what I am in actuality. I was in search of myself, in fact.

In the event I also made discoveries that affected my understanding of my grandparents. And not only that; in Finland I discovered a lot about the America that they had arrived in and in which I lived. I began to understand my father better. I saw how history has shaped who we are. And I learned something of what it means to be a Finn.

So I sent my letter to Aino Ahonen. My father had told me that she could understand English but that it was best to keep it simple. He said that her reply would be full of mistakes but comprehensible. Sometimes, he said, she used a Finnish word, hoping that he, my father, would know it. 'She might do the same with you,' he said and grinned. That grin really puzzled me. For a long time I couldn't find how to interpret it; but I did eventually, it was a nervous grin. 'If she does, you can show it to me. I might be able to drag it out of my memory,' he added.

I waited quite a while for a reply, several weeks, as I remember. And when it did arrive, it wasn't from Aino but from someone called Päivi, whose surname was also Makinen. She'd put those two dots over the 'a' in Makinen as well, like in Päivi. I knew it was some kind of accent, of course, though I didn't know what effect it would produce. I must confess that I didn't bother to use those dots myself whenever I wrote her name. I guess they would have been on my keyboard somewhere, but I didn't know how to find them then, and in her email address the dots weren't used so it wasn't a problem.

The letter explained that she was Aino's second cousin and that Aino had passed my letter on to her. It was written in faultless English which made me feel quite ashamed of the scrappily composed message that I had sent. Päivi mentioned that she was an English teacher in high school, so that explained it. She said that she welcomed this chance to exchange letters with a native English speaker and the opportunity it would afford her of practicing her English. It did sound dreadfully formal, if perfectly correct. And I'll admit up-front that the formality was a bit off-putting. I imagined a prim schoolmistress in a high-necked blouse and tortoiseshell glasses.

However, I was the suppliant, asking for favors and information, and certainly far more inclined to be grateful for the time she had taken to reply and the offer contained in her letter, to provide what help and information she could about her side of my grandparents' family. Päivi had also supplied an email address, which was a relief as it saved time and I found letter-writing arduous.

So it was that I established contact with my Finnish relatives. Over the following months, Päivi provided me with the information to complete the Makinen side of the family tree from the parents of my grandfather down to the present day. Since Päivi was Aino's second cousin, which was the same relation that Aino was to me, it meant, of course, that Päivi and I were also second cousins. Aino, Päivi and myself each had one grandparent who had been siblings. This knowledge made me feel very close to these women I had never met, who lived on the other side of the world. About my grandmother's family, the Virtanens, Päivi wasn't able to tell me anything, though. Any connections between the Virtanens and Makinens had not survived my grandparents' departure to America.

As each new name, date of birth, marriage, death was added to my family tree I felt my enthusiasm for the whole project increasing. I discovered some interesting facts, too, that fired my interest further. My grandfather had had a twin brother, named Arto, something that I hadn't known before. Neither had my father, apparently, which suggested pretty strongly to me that my grandparents must have had some reason for wishing to bury that part of the past. That twin brother had died in 1918, just two years before my grandparents had emigrated. When my own father was christened Arto, he was receiving the name of his father's dead twin. It suggested that my grandfather was perhaps trying, in some subconscious or primitive way, to compensate for the loss of the first Arto.

Furthermore, the Juho that my grandparents were so fond of, their nephew, was born in 1918, the same year that Arto died. Did they feel that the new baby somehow replaced the lost brother? Was that why they felt the special bond my father had spoken of? It seemed quite likely, even probable. I wondered how the older Arto had died. He would have been only twenty-three years old. I asked Päivi in one of my emails but she forgot, or neglected, to provide that piece of information amongst all the other queries I was sending her and I didn't mention it again in case there was some particular reason why she, too, had wished to avoid the topic.

My impression of Päivi underwent considerable revision during this time. She soon dropped the formality. Perhaps email helped. And also getting past the first contact. Päivi was born, she told me, in 1957, so she was one year younger than me. She'd been married and was divorced. Her two children, a boy and a girl, Anni and Toni, were already away from home, studying at university. She also explained that when she married, she had not taken her husband's name but had kept her own. That was an option in Finland, she wrote, and that was one reason why she was still called Makinen. The other, she added, was that she would have reverted to it anyway, had she taken her husband's name on marriage. She put an exclamation mark after that, which I duly took note of.

We started sending photos by email, first of ourselves and immediate family, then of other relatives. There weren't so many that I could send that would interest Päivi, but she sent me pictures of some of the relatives that she was supplying dates and information about, so I was able to put faces to names and that brought the exercise much more to life for me. Päivi herself was nothing like I'd imagined. She was small and slim, with straight, darkish hair, cut in a simple way, a sort of grown-out page-boy style. Not at all prim.

My imagination was so much stimulated by the results of my investigations and the new perspective it was giving me on my family and roots that, within a few months of the start, I began to be more aware of the growth of my desire to visit the country, to see the places where these names on the family tree had lived and worked and died. I wanted to bring those names to life and being where they had spent their lives seemed like the way to try to do that. I realized, too, that in order to gather information about my grandmother's family, and to go further back in history on both sides, I would need to study the parish registers in the villages where my forefathers had lived.

The notion of visiting Finland took hold of me like a fever and I was pretty soon running a high temperature. I was distracted. I couldn't concentrate on my duties at the college library where I work. I could barely sit still at home. There were rows because I was so entirely absorbed in this other world that was opening up before me. Helen, my wife, was perfectly justified in taking exception to the extent to which my family history project dominated my attention. I make no excuses. I admit that I was becoming obsessed, and obsession is not an easy state to be around, much less to live with. The boys simply avoided me most of the time. They had their own interests and affairs to occupy them and take them out of the house, so in a way it was easier for them to deal with the situation. But between Helen and me it was becoming a problem.

Finally, we had a big discussion during which I presented to Helen my idea that I would travel to Finland the next summer to do all the research on location that I couldn't do from America and didn't feel that I could ask Päivi to do for me. She'd already donated a lot of time to interviewing her elderly relatives, collecting facts and then writing the results up to send to me.

Helen received the idea coldly. 'How long will you need in Finland to do all this?' she asked. I, of course, couldn't estimate at all how time-consuming it would be. In a sense, these projects are endless. There's always an earlier generation or another family branch to follow. However, it was not just a question of how long it needed. My time was not unlimited. I reckoned that I'd be able to negotiate enough time off work to spend three weeks in Finland, the summer being quiet in the college library, but I wouldn't get any more than that.

'And what am I supposed to do while you go off with your Payvee,' (Helen had an exaggerated way of pronouncing the end of her name that was supposed to convey disapprobation, though she had nothing whatsoever to base such an attitude on), 'searching through dusty records?' Helen wanted to know, not unreasonably.

'You could come along, too,' I said.

'I'm not interested, Len. I know who my family are. And I don't want to be dragged round a lot of your long-lost relatives, people I don't know and I'm not interested in and who probably don't speak English.'

I could see that it didn't look like a bright prospect for Helen and, to be honest, I had expected strong resistance to the whole idea from her. However, I was quite determined in my own mind to carry out my project and was equally serious about finding the best solution that would suit us both. So I approached the question in a very calm, logical and - what I think must have been very clear in my way of speaking and general behavior - a determined fashion. Unusually for me, I should add: determination is not one of my typical characteristics. I reckon that something new in my manner must have gotten through to Helen and caused her, perhaps subconsciously, to tread a little warily. Although she made her lack of enthusiasm quite plain, she left a space for compromise.

First, we considered whether there could be some activity that would engage her while my time was occupied, but there was nothing that we could come up with. Then we considered that she might be based in another country in Europe, Italy maybe, or England, doing stuff that interested her while I went to Finland. Then we could meet up and do some things together before travelling back to the States. But this idea fell flat. There wasn't anything that Helen wanted to do on her own, nor any place in Europe where she might have wanted to do it, if there had been.

'I'd rather stay in America,' she said flatly.

'And I really want to get a trip to Finland, ' I countered.

'Well …?'

'So are you happy staying here while I go on my family research trip?'

And that's how it was decided that I would travel alone to Finland the following summer. It was still before Christmas when we had this conversation. Maybe, since the realization of the plan was still quite distant, Helen didn't fully believe in its actuality. Maybe she had the idea that when the time drew closer, something would happen to prevent it. Perhaps she thought that I would just change my mind, lose the overriding interest that I'd had in the whole project. Whatever the reason was, as summer approached, with my travel plans made and no sign of change on the horizon, Helen's attitude became distinctly hostile. At first she withdrew, becoming uncommunicative, answering questions with a monosyllable. You know those ghastly mealtimes that pass in silence except for the click and scrape of cutlery on the plate? Well, we had plenty of those. And a few rows when the issue of what she was going to do during my absence came up.

'I don't know, Len. And you don't have to pretend you're interested,' was the response I got to my enquiries, so I pretty soon stopped asking.

If she'd thought that these tactics would wear me down and lead me to cancel my trip, though, she was wrong. I remained adamant.

Well, I don't want to dwell on the situation. We'd had rows before and differences of opinion. Doesn't every marriage? Somehow, one way or another, we'd always ridden the storm. With the passage of time the issue at the center of the conflict became less important and was eventually forgotten. I assumed the same would happen on this occasion, too. In the meantime, I just dug in my heels and waited for summer.

Chapter Three

I had timed my trip to Finland to coincide with Päivi's summer holiday. That was easily done because, being a school teacher, she had a long summer break. I didn't expect her to devote all her time to me while I was in Finland, of course. However, she'd insisted that she would be happy to show me around, introduce me to some of her, and my, relatives, and, what was most important, accompany me on trips to those villages where the earlier Makinens and the Virtanens had lived. I would be dependent on her Finnish to obtain information from the parish records.

After I'd registered my surprise at the temperature on arrival, I got myself a taxi to my hotel in the center of town. I'd planned a couple of days on my own in Helsinki before traveling to Päivi's hometown of Hämeenlinna, about 60 miles to the north. I wanted to do a bit of sight-seeing, but also, knowing myself so well, I knew that I would be jet-lagged and wanted some time to get over it. So I breakfasted at four in the afternoon and was ready to order my dinner just as the nightclubs were closing. Luckily, my hotel had a 24-hour restaurant.

Little-by-little I tried to adjust to the local time. I wandered round the city, taking in the atmosphere, sitting in cafes, listening to the language, trying to catch its rhythms and to gauge the sense from the tone and inflection of the voices. People mainly sounded angry, so I hoped that I was failing. I enjoyed sitting in the Esplanade park, watching the people go by, and walking along the Esplanade, down to the harbor to watch the boats and the sunlight sparkling on the waves. There were many jetties with private sailing boats and cruisers and, on the far side of the harbor, a terminal for large ferry boats.

At the end of the Esplanade, beside the harbor, there was an open, cobbled area with a lively outdoor market selling fresh vegetables, fish and hand-crafted wooden bowls, and various items that tourists might like to buy. There were also several large tents operating as cafes where you could buy coffee and snacks. Along the quayside next to this market area there was a row of small wooden kiosks with boards advertising boat trips of varying length and itinerary. I selected a trip around the coastal waters and out to a small island one afternoon.

These waterways were pretty busy. A constant stream of small boats was coming and going, the surface of the sea continuously choppy from their bow waves. There was a small sandy beach on the island and low, smooth, almost flat rocks at either end of it, and on a warm and sunny afternoon it was full of sunbathers and swimmers, with the buildings of downtown Helsinki making an attractive skyline about a mile away across the water.

Walking back from the Esplanade to my hotel on my first afternoon in Helsinki I passed an impressive-looking, neo-classical building which turned out to be the Finnish National Gallery. I decided to go in and have a wander round. My expectations were not that great. I realized I wouldn't find anything to rival the famous art galleries of Europe, obviously, but I assumed there would be a small selection of well-known European painters, padded out with some lesser-known artists. Enough to occupy an hour or so quite pleasantly without being too demanding.

Now I'm no art critic and I make no claims to expert knowledge. I enjoy visiting art galleries and I've read up a bit about art history in the western tradition; enough to know the major names, identify some of the most important styles and movements, and to recognize a handful of famous paintings. In the Finnish National Gallery I learned that my kind of superficial acquaintance with western painting excludes entirely the products of Finnish artists. Had I been asked, before my visit, to name a Finnish painter, I would have been unable to do so. I would probably have assumed that whatever Finnish painters there are, they do not rank with the European and American greats. Whatever 'rank' means here. I'm damned if I know. Maybe there are people who can judge. Earlier I would have unquestioningly assumed that there were and that my short-list of big names was firmly based on their sound judgment. Now I'm less sure.

From the cool, dim entrance foyer I made my way up the wide stone stairs to the second floor and entered a fairly large room; the largest in the gallery, as it turned out, though moderately-sized compared with the most prestigious galleries. Every painting was by a Finnish artist. That was the first surprise.

I stopped before a medium-sized canvas of three young boys on the sea shore. 'Albert Edelfelt: Boys Playing on the Beach, 1884'. The horizon was closed in by a distant shoreline of low hills and forest, but there were a couple of sea-going ships on the water so this must have been a coastal inlet. The boys were playing with toy boats, balancing on rocks in the shallows, one reaching out with a stick to guide his boat. They appeared wholly absorbed in their game, their backs to the real ships in the distance. That was the adult world that they were unconsciously moving towards, their games mimicking it and in a way, perhaps, preparing them to enter it eventually. The whole scene was full of light and life, the positions of the boys suggestive of movement, yet the atmosphere was calm and unhurried. I wanted to say 'innocent' but I'm not sure that's the right word.

Moving on I noticed a picture that put me in mind, on first glance, of paintings in the arcadian pastoral tradition with their romanticized landscapes and classical buildings on distant cliff tops. I stepped closer and read, 'Hjalmar Munsterhjelm: Forest Pond by Moonlight, 1881'. My first impression was not quite right. This landscape was rugged, but not so romanticized. A full moon appeared in the middle of the sky, brightly illuminating some scattered clouds. A path of moonlight crossed the pond in the foreground, moonlight caught spots of dew on vegetation. Rocks and boulders surrounded the pond, then dense pine forest covered the hills, a mist rising between the trunks that gradually swallowed up the form of the trees as they receded into the valley in the background. There were no buildings, classical or otherwise, no signs of human habitation at all. The scene was quite wild, desolate even.

I stood dreamily in front of this picture, imagining that I was stepping across the wet foreground undergrowth to the edge of the pond – the effect of my jetlag, probably. I half-closed my eyes and conjured the brilliance of the full moon, the tips of the pines silhouetted in rows, like the teeth of a saw, against the brightness. And something seemed to be calling out to me. At first I took no notice. Or rather, I thought it was the middle ground of the painting, the lighted area on the other side of the pond, beyond the moonpath, leading into the forest that was inviting me into the scene.

But gradually I became aware of something on the periphery of my perception, drawing my attention. The color of the pond repeated, a figure. I turned slightly and looked directly towards the painting that had been insinuating its way into my consciousness, calling for me to notice it. It showed a girl or young woman whose figure occupied a large part of the canvas. She was standing in a field holding the long wooden handle of some farming implement; a rake, perhaps. Beyond the field, but not so distant, was the edge of the forest. The girl's head was above the line of the tree tops, in profile against the luminosity of the sky that echoed the moonlight reflected on the forest pond. The girl's head was raised and slightly back and her mouth was wide open in the act of calling out vigorously.

I went over to the picture. 'Ellen Thesleff: The Echo, 1891'. There were no other figures in view. The echo, the loud call, and the return of the caller's voice. Solitude. Solitary. I stood there and tried to hear the echo.

I began to feel excited. I'd been in a sort of trance from the moment I'd stepped into this first room. This wasn't what I'd expected at all and I'd been surprised and immediately captivated. Now a sense of urgency came over me, which was not very logical since I had plenty of time and no need to hurry, but put it down to the excitement. I had covered less than half of that first room, but I found myself beside the door into the next and passed through, thinking that I could return later. It was as if I was afraid of missing something.

The first thing that caught my eye in the second room was a medium-sized canvas with a very pale background and a figure occupying the foreground. It was a winter scene. The background was a snow-covered landscape, dead flat, a frozen lake perhaps, and a wintery sky. On the horizon was a narrow strip of land, very distant, presumably the far shore of the lake. The figure in the foreground, who dominated the picture, was a soldier, slumped against the trunk of a silver birch tree, his knapsack behind him, his hat on the snow. He supported himself with one arm, his other hand clutched a rifle with bayonet fixed. His uniform was from the Napoleonic period.

I checked the notice beside the painting. 'Helene Schjerfbeck: A Wounded Soldier, 1880'. His head lolled uncomfortably to his left but his eyes were open, his expression appeared calm. Half-way across the lake and too

31

distant to make out any details, the receding column of his comrades could be seen. The wounded soldier was not looking towards them but gazing with a faraway look towards a point at right angles to where they marched. His hair was fair, cut short and tidy. His skin was fair, smooth and clean, a slight pinkness on his cheek. He looked like a schoolboy as he lay there, waiting to die.

There were other Schjerfbeck paintings, a series of self-portraits representing the artist at different stages of her life and painted in an increasingly minimalist and abstract style as she became older. In the last, painted in old age, the body seemed almost to have become refined into something semi-corporeal, almost transparent and lacking individual features.

Further on I stopped to contemplate 'Eero Järnefelt: Children Playing, 1895', which showed the completely naked figures of a boy and girl, aged about eleven or twelve, I'd guess. Their two figures almost filled the canvas. The girl was red-haired and lying on her back on the grass with her legs parted and bent and her right arm raised above her head. The boy was crouched beside her, his left knee planted on the ground between her legs, his right arm behind her head was gripping her raised right arm. His hips and buttocks were raised up and his left hand appeared to be holding her left hand pinned to her stomach and his head and upper torso were lowered over it. They appeared to be engaged in a friendly wrestling match. The girl's face was fully visible and she was smiling. The boy's face was hidden. If they'd been ten years older, it would have been a painting of lovers. Actually, if they'd been five years older. The girl was holding a small ball, like a tennis ball, in her raised right hand. The boy seemed to be trying to get it from her and she was resisting. It might have been an apple.

I came next to another picture of naked children; 'Verner Thomé: Boys Playing on a Sandy Beach, 1904'. The sand and the three figures of the boys filled the canvas, there was no sky. The entire picture was composed of different shades and tones of the same color, yellow-brown. It did for the sand and the skin of the boys. Where the sand or their skin reflected the direct sunlight, the tone was a whitish-yellow glare. Two of the boys sprawled on the sand, the third crouched beside them. The painting was suffused with light and heat. The boys' bodies seemed to be made of the same material as the ground they lay on, as if they had been molded from it.

So I moved through the gallery, from room to room, stopping before some paintings, moving past others. Scenes of Finnish landscape were prominent; lake scenery, views from hilltops over forest, valleys and water, small holdings and houses, land cleared from the forest for farming, rivers and rapids, in all the four seasons.

Finally, I returned to the large room where I'd started and where I'd left more than half the pictures unviewed. I glanced at a Parisian street scene and an opera scene, both done in what looked like an impressionist style to me. They could have been painted by Renoir or Manet to my inexpert eye. I checked the sign beside the paintings. Both were by Akseli Gallen-Kallela. Beside them was a painting of a half-rotten fish washed up on the edge of a stony shore. It was done in dark and subdued colors, something between naturalism and impressionism. 'Akseli Gallen-Kallela: Rotting Fish, 1884'. Even half decomposed I could identify it as a walleye.

My attention was now caught by a fairly large, bright canvas. It was approximately twice as high as it was wide and the subject was a wild flower in its natural setting. The flower was close up in the foreground and occupied almost the whole of the canvas from top to bottom. The treatment

33

was very clear and sharp, not quite photo-realism, but tending that way. Behind the plant, and visible between the stems, leaves and flowers was a typical Finnish lake and forest scene. The colors were bright. The sky was a pale blue, the lake an almost unreal cobalt blue, as if the quality of the light and clarity of the air gave nature these vivid tones and sharp outlines. I checked the artist. Akseli Gallen-Kallela again: 'Wild Angelica, 1889'.

I moved on and came next to a painting in a completely different style: modernist or expressionist, perhaps. It represented a young woman standing on a rock beside water holding a baby against her breast. The background consisted of rocks and trees. There was the faintest suggestion of a halo round the woman's head and the expression on her face was one of serious contemplation shading into sadness. The sign read, 'Akseli Gallen-Kallela: Marjatta by the Waterside, 1896'. I could hardly believe that this painting could also be by the same artist who had painted the impressionist-style Parisian scenes and the realist flower and landscape. 1896 seemed very early to me for such a modern piece of work.

Beside Marjatta was another painting of a waterside scene. Here the water was almost black and a ghostly swan, its white dimmed by shadow, floated on the water. The naked corpse of a man lay on the shore and an elderly woman crouched beside him, her face turned upward to the sky. There was a skull and some bones in the foreground and a few highly stylized flowers grew from the stony ground. At first I'd thought they were candles placed in ornate holders. Rocks along the water's edge were covered with splodges of bright orange lichen that suggested blood. The whole composition was clearly heavily symbolic though I was unable to read the symbolism and the style tended towards expressionism, I thought, except for the woman's face which had been given

34

a naturalist treatment. There was a confidence and determination in the woman's expression and she looked as if she was waiting for something. Her hand rested on the man's breast. Perhaps he was not dead. Perhaps she was trying to heal him, confident of her power to do so but waiting for some vital medicine, or for her power to take effect. It was an odd and haunting picture. I checked the sign; 'Akseli Gallen-Kallela; Lemminkainen's Mother, 1897'.

Turning, I saw a painting on the adjacent wall that looked to me rather out of place, even amongst this heterogeneous collection of work. The composition, at first glance, made me think of the album cover of a progressive rock band. It represented a naked young woman with her arms opened wide and slightly raised, with a night sky and stars behind her and a huge moon. Her hair was spread out in a circle around her head, like flames. A layer of cloud swirled around her thighs.

'That, at least, can't be by Gallen-Kallela,' I murmured to myself as I approached the painting. I leant towards the sign and read; 'Akseli Gallen-Kallela: Ad Astra, 1907'. From that point on I decided that this guy could probably paint anything, in any style. I took a closer look at Ad Astra and noticed that the woman's hands, the palms facing outward to the viewer, were marked with the stigmata: a female Christ.

I left the Finnish National Gallery in thoughtful mood, turning over in my mind the images that I'd been looking at, trying to process and begin to understand what I'd seen and how it had affected me. I felt as if I'd been through some kind of initiation, a baptism by art. During the three weeks that I spent in Finland, these pictures and images would from time to time surface in my mind. Places and experiences would evoke one or other of these pictures and sometimes I found that I was looking at a scene, or a detail in it, or considering a particular event, as if it was the subject of a painting. It was as if my experience was being mediated by art.

Chapter Four

By the second day in Helsinki I was beginning to find my way around and discovered some interesting places and sights. I found a nice little cafe where I could get excellent coffee and interesting sweet buns and cakes. It was in the courtyard of a Jugend style building on a quiet street near the center of town and was decorated in a totally idiosyncratic manner. No two tables were the same size and each was covered with a different, brightly colored tablecloth. Each of the chairs had a gentleman's suit vest over the back and each vest was designed in vivid colors, many with sequins. There was an unusual collection of disparate objects decorating the walls, shelves and other surfaces. Jazz music played in the background.

I was served by a Russian waitress. I judged her to be Russian from her accent. Of course, Russia is very close to Helsinki. There's a very long border between the two countries. I don't know why I should have been surprised to meet a Russian waitress in Helsinki. I think I'd gotten the idea that Russians were not often met with outside Russia. An attitude left over from cold war and Soviet days, I suppose. The world is changing, let's hope for the better.

The light in Helsinki made a big impression on me. I don't mean so much the light during the middle of the day, though that did have a quality that was new to me and which I would describe as gentle. But more than that, it was the length of the daylight hours. At midnight it was barely dusk; by four in the morning, if there was not too much cloud cover, the sky was fully bright. Minnesota, where I live, has a climate that's very similar to Finland, I now realize, in terms of temperature and rain and snowfall, but it's the product of our mid-continental location, rather than latitude. Minnesota is considerably further south so we don't get those light nights in the summertime. It was also the reason why I'd assumed Finland would have colder summers than Minnesota. But that light sure didn't help me to adjust my internal clock.

However, after my two days in Helsinki, and with the ability to stay awake, at least, between mid-day and seven in the evening, I set off for Hämeenlinna. I traveled by train. I'd originally planned to hire a car for the whole of my stay but when I'd mentioned this to Päivi, she'd been dead against it. 'It's so expensive and such a waste of money,' she'd written in her email, 'and completely pointless when I have a car that would just be standing there unused, if we both went in your rental car.'

Well, it made sense, even though I couldn't help feeling like I was imposing on her. It also suggested that Päivi herself was picturing that we'd be moving about together most of the time, so perhaps I didn't need to worry too much about imposing. Finally, we agreed that we would use her car if she let me pay all the gasoline costs. If I felt that things weren't working out that way, I could always hire a car for some of the time once I was in Finland.

We had arranged that Päivi would meet me at the railroad station. 'Beside the kiosk selling magazines and sweets, just inside the main door,' she'd instructed. I'd gotten the picture of a large and busy mainline station with crowds of people milling around, that made this exact meeting point necessary, but in fact it was so small and almost empty that we couldn't possibly have missed each other.

I'll confess to feeling both nervous and excited as the train slowed on its approach to the station. I'd already gotten used to the idea of having Finnish relatives and being able to put names to their faces in photographs, and I'd established a comfortable written relationship with Päivi. But the first face-to-face meeting, that was something special and significant. It felt like entering a new area of my life. I mean 'area'. It's not a misprint of 'era', and I don't mean 'phase', either. Those are temporal words that suggest that this space was just now coming into existence. But it was a space that had always been there, I had just never entered it before.

I spotted Päivi the moment I came through the door into the station hall, standing right beside the kiosk, just like she'd said. She was wearing a yellowish t-shirt, beige pants that ended half-way down her calf, and leather sandals on bare feet. She looked even more slight than she had done in the photos she sent me. Her figure was so slim it was almost girlish. She sure didn't look her forty-three years. Like I said, I couldn't have missed her. I went straight over to her. 'Hi,' I announced, 'I'm Len Makinen.'

A movement flickered over Päivi's lips, almost like an involuntary, nervous twitch which she seemed to control and replace with a real smile. 'Hello,' she said. 'I'm Päivi.'

She pronounced her name a bit differently to how I was used to saying it. There was a short silence. I was sort of waiting for Päivi to take the lead, I guess, but she seemed to be waiting, too. Then she made an odd sound, like a suppressed laugh that had escaped.

'Is something wrong?' I asked. 'Have I put my foot in it right at the start?'

'Oh no. I'm sorry, Len. It's just the way you said our family name. You made it sound like a Scottish name; Mc something-or-other. It's not pronounced like that in Finnish. It's Mäkinen. The stress is on the first syllable, "Mäk", which is pronounced like "smack" but without the "s". Then a short "in" and a short "en". Mäkinen.'

'Okay. I'd better learn to say it right, pretty sharpish. It wouldn't look good if I couldn't pronounce my own name,' I said humorously. 'And it's real nice to meet you at last,

39

Päivi.' I made a special effort to imitate the way that she had pronounced her name.

'Oh Len, it's wonderful to meet you, too. I'm so glad... We're *all* so glad, that you made contact after all these years.' And she put her arms round me and gave me a big hug. I'd have done the same, meeting family or friends back in Minnesota, but it was a real surprise coming from Päivi. I'd thought Finns didn't hug as a greeting. And right at that moment I had ... well, I don't know whether to call it a memory or a feeling, but I guess it was a bit of both, that my grandparents never had hugged me as a child.

'I'm sorry I laughed at the way you said our name,' she added, right after the hug. 'I shouldn't have done that. I don't like it when people laugh because of the way foreigners pronounce words or names in their language. It took me by surprise, though. I wasn't expecting it and I tried not to laugh, but it forced its way out. I hope you aren't angry.'

'No, of course not. I'm not so thin-skinned.' And I gave her what I hoped was a reassuring grin.

'And anyway, it's your name, too, not just mine. If it's pronounced McKinnon in America then that's your name. You have every right to say it the way you want.'

'I guess I'll keep saying it as before in the States, but while I'm here in Finland I want to have a real Finnish surname.'

We collected up my luggage then and went out to the car park where I loaded it into the trunk of Päivi's car.

'You said in your emails that you do not speak any Finnish,' Päivi said, once we were on the road and heading towards my hotel in the town center. 'But didn't you learn any Finnish words as a child?'

I explained that my grandfather had told me the names of some common objects and a few other things but that I'd forgotten many of them.

'Tell me one of the words that you remember.'

I searched through my memory for a word, but it had gone blank, as it usually does when I'm unexpectedly asked to remember something from the past. At last, I managed to draw a word up from the depths.

'Well, the word "sota" means war. Did I say it right?'

'Not really. You make it sound like the end of Minnesota. The stress should be at the beginning. It is in all Finnish words. The first syllable is like sock without the "ck". The letter "a" is always pronounced like the "u" in bus, except when it has the two dots above it, of course. Then it's pronounced like the "a" in cat, as in Mäkinen. So, the Finnish word for "war" is pronounced "so-ta". I wonder why he taught you that word? Did he ever talk to you about the war?'

'Not that I remember. But I was only eleven when he died. Which war is *the* war, in this case? The First World War, I suppose.'

'No, I was thinking of the civil war.'

'Oh, right.' I must have sounded a bit uncertain.

'Do you know about our civil war, Len?'

'I'm ashamed to admit that my knowledge of Finnish history is pretty hazy. I know Finland was once part of the old Russian Empire and became independent in 1917 after the Russian Revolution. I thought that process was quite peaceful in Finland, but was there fighting between Finland and the Russian Bolsheviks? Is that what you mean by civil war?'

'Not really, but you have got the right period. After the Russian Revolution, the Finnish people themselves were divided between the red, communist side and the white, right-wing side, and they fought a very bloody war for several months in 1918. The white side won.'

'1918? That was not long before my grandparents left Finland; only two years.'

'That's why I wondered if he had ever talked to you about it.'

At that point we arrived at my hotel and that topic was broken off as Päivi parked and I unloaded my luggage.

Chapter Five

Hämeenlinna is a pretty small town and although my hotel was one of the main ones in the town center, it was still modest compared with American city-center hotels. Päivi waited in the middle of the foyer beside my bags while I checked in at the reception and she was only half a dozen paces away, so that gives you an idea of the size of the place. When I'd gotten my key-card I stepped over to where she was standing.

'Would you like to have dinner at my flat this evening, Len?' she asked, and then quickly added, 'Only if you want to. If you are tired and want to rest up today, just say so.'

I assured her that I hadn't come to Finland to sit in a hotel room, and I felt quite confident that I could keep the remains of the jet-lag away until a reasonable hour in the evening.

'That's great. We can have a nice long chat and get to know each other properly. There is one other thing. Is it okay if we go to see my mother before eating? She's very keen to meet you, even though she cannot say more than one or two words in English.'

'Absolutely,' I told her. 'I'm keen to meet your mother, too, and say my two words in Finnish.'

I was kind of surprised at myself saying 'absolutely' like that. I sounded like an Englishman. Päivi's English was not only pretty well faultless, but she spoke it just like a real Brit and I figured that I was subconsciously imitating her style of speech in some small ways. I hoped she wouldn't think I was doing it deliberately. I sure hadn't lost my Minnesota accent, though. I could hear that well enough. I almost asked Päivi how she came to sound so English, but somehow it felt a bit nosey, having just met her. I was a bit afraid she might think I was getting a dig back at her because she commented on my pronunciation of our family name. I sure didn't want her to think that, so I said nothing.

Anyway, we agreed that Päivi would leave me at my hotel for a couple of hours so I could freshen up, and then she came back to pick me up and drove me to her apartment. Since her mother lived so close, we left the car at Päivi's place and walked the few hundred yards to get there. We stayed for an hour or so, drinking coffee and eating cake and biscuits. Marja, Päivi's mother, looked quite elderly, with her shock of untidy grey hair and short, dumpy figure. She moved rather awkwardly, as if her legs or feet were painful. I knew from the family tree that she was actually sixty-seven, but she looked a good deal older. Marja lived alone. Päivi's father, Erkki, had died a few years before. She'd had a brother too, Esko, who had died just two years ago, at the age of only forty-three.

Marja had a lot of questions which she addressed to Päivi, of course, who translated them to me and then translated my answer back to her. Marja was very talkative but scarcely looked at me the whole time. It was as if she was holding a conversation with Päivi alone and I was not there. It was an odd experience for me, and the first time that I had ever been like that in a foreign language environment, but there was nothing I could do about it, not knowing the language. And I guess it couldn't have been any other way, really.

When we left, Päivi suggested that we take a short detour on the way back to her place that would take us through the center of the town. We'd driven that route earlier when Päivi had picked me up from the station and taken me to my hotel, but of course I hadn't been able to get much of an impression of the place from the car. She led me along a couple of residential streets and into a central square. There were trees and benches around the square and a neo-classical building on one side that I would have put at late nineteenth century.

'That is our town hall,' Päivi informed me.

We walked on and pretty quickly arrived back at Päivi's place. It was a small apartment in a modern block. By American standards, it was actually very small, a couple of rooms, kitchen and bathroom, and a room not much bigger than a cupboard, which Päivi called her study. The kitchen was very modern and the whole place was nicely appointed and functional, but I couldn't help the word 'modest' springing into my mind again, like with the hotel, every time I let my eyes wander round the accommodation on that first day. Marja's apartment had produced a similar impression. It may have been coincidence, but all of the apartments that I visited during my stay in Finland had the same quality, all of them afforded what seemed to me decidedly cramped quarters.

I knew that Päivi's father and brother had died not long before. There'd also been a sister who died as an infant. She'd given me the dates for the family tree in our email correspondence, but she hadn't gone into any details and I hadn't asked about the circumstances. I actually knew very little about her personal history beyond those bare dates and the fact of her divorce. Later, over dinner, I asked about her childhood.

'Were you born in Hämeenlinna, Päivi?' I began.

'No, I was born in Lahti, in the hospital there, and I grew up in Hämeenkoski.'

'I know where Lahti is, from the map,' I said, 'but I don't know Hämeenkoski.'

'I'm not surprised. It's a small village about half way between Hämeenlinna and Lahti. I will show you,' and she went to get a map and pointed out Hämeenlinna, Hämeenkoski and Lahti, pretty much on a straight line of

45

some forty or fifty miles from west to east, about sixty miles north of Helsinki.

'It must be pretty rural. Was your father a farmer?' I asked, remembering my grandmother's photo.

'It was rural, yes, and there was a lot of agriculture in the area, but we were not a farming family. My father started in construction work and later worked as a kind of technician in a small engineering firm.'

As we continued to look at the map, Päivi pointed to a large lake that stretched north from Lahti.

'That's Päijänne, ' she said. 'That's where I spent my summer holidays with my family as a child. We used to build a camp on this island, called Kelvenne. Here,' and she pointed to a long, narrow island in the middle of the lake. It was about ten miles long but barely half a mile wide at its widest point.

'The island is actually the top of a sand and gravel ridge, most of which is submerged, that is why it's that shape. There are lovely sandy beaches all along the shore and we used to build our camp beside one. A little way beyond the end of the beach there were two small but very deep lagoons where the water was so dark it was almost black. They had sandy edges, too, that sloped down very steeply. They were such mysterious places.'

'It sounds lovely; idyllic.'

'It was. We used to go with my uncle Juhani and aunt Raili, who were really my father's aunt and uncle. They lived near Lahti and had a boat. It was a wooden boat, very wide in the middle and pointed at each end and it rolled in the water. We used to call it the fat boat. It had one of those inboard motors that make a "putt-putt" noise. Juhani built the boat himself. He was very clever like that, and the boat and the lake were his great interest. And Raili's, too. They both loved to go boating and fishing and they used to take us to Kelvenne. I remember it so well. We none of us had a car in those days. So me, Esko, and my parents travelled by bus to Lahti, to the boat place, with all our equipment: mattresses, clothes, plastic sheets, food supplies …'

'Did you say plastic sheets?' I interrupted. 'What did you need them for?'

'To build the camp. We didn't have any tents, you see. The men cut long poles from the branches of trees on the island and then they built a frame that they covered with large plastic sheets. And we put plastic sheets on the ground, too, for the mattresses to go on. I remember we made it like home, with all sorts of practical additions, like hooks, and there were poles inside, too, where we could hang clothes and other things. There were jars of wild flowers that we had collected, hanging outside the hut. We had a separate kitchen building, too, constructed in the same way but with only three walls and one side completely open. There was a little stove inside it. You know one of those metal stoves on legs which you light a fire inside. Like a miniature kitchen range. That must have been on the boat already because I'm sure we didn't carry that with us on the bus. And we also had an open fire with a metal grid over it for grilling.'

'Did you take the kitchen sink?' I asked, with a smile.

'Almost,' Päivi replied. 'We even took a big tin full of worms to use for fishing because it was impossible to find them on Kelvenne, the earth was too sandy. It was quite an adventure. We were really loaded up with all our stuff on the bus ride to Lahti. All the clothes we needed, because it could be cold some days, especially at night. And food supplies. We must have looked quite a sight,' she said with a laugh.

'And there weren't any shops on the island?'

'Heavens, no! There weren't any buildings at all. No one lived on Kelvenne.'

47

'So you had to take all your food with you. How long did you stay there?'

'We were there for three or four weeks. The whole of my father's summer holiday. Yes, we took food with us - fresh vegetables, lots of potatoes, dried foods like porridge and pasta, tinned meat, vegetables and fruit. I remember that we children had to eat porridge every morning. We were not allowed to go and play until we'd eaten our porridge. It's quite a tradition in Finland. Or at least, it used to be. A lot of people cannot stand the sight of the stuff because they had to eat so much of it as children. We often had tinned pea soup because it was easy to store and prepare and it's very filling and nutritious. We did not eat rice in those days; it's become popular in Finland since then. And we caught fish from the lake, of course. We ate a lot of fish because there was always a good supply of it: fish soup, grilled fish, salted fish, smoked fish. We had a smoking box with us.'

'What did you do for drinking water?'

'We took that with us. We had several large plastic containers full of drinking water. They were already on Juhani's boat; we didn't carry them with us on the bus. They would have been much too heavy. We were able to refill the containers as they became empty at the boat service stations dotted around the shore. We used the lake water for washing and for cooking. We boiled the cooking water first to be sure it was clean.'

'Didn't it make the food taste muddy?'

'Not so far as I remember,' she replied. 'The lake water was pretty clean. I might be a bit more discerning today, though. We always had a big lunch in the early afternoon. That was the main meal of the day and preparing it occupied the women for half the morning. In the evening we often made pancakes over the fire. That was always the men's job. My father made a mean pancake. Oh, I loved those pancakes and the smell of them cooking. I can still smell it now.

'But we did go shopping, too. Some things, like milk, we had to get fresh, although we also used powdered milk when the fresh ran out. But about once a week we went by boat to the nearest village on the shore to top up our supplies. As I remember, we used to get the shopping in the rowing boat. I think that would have been because Juhani and Raili often left Kelvenne to go boating somewhere else for a few days, and they would leave their boat's dinghy behind for us to use until they came back. Their children, Mari and Liisa, usually stayed on the island with us. They had other relatives and friends around the shore of Lake Päijänne that they used to go visiting. And they just loved to be in their boat. They were off cruising for more time than they spent on the island. Sometimes they would take me with them on a visit and I had my own triangular shaped cabin in the front of the boat. I loved it so much.'

'So you were marooned on a desert island,' I joked.

'Yes. Or, well, not really marooned because we had the dinghy although it was not really big enough for all of us, especially in later years when my other uncle and aunt and cousins came, too. We couldn't all get in the dinghy then. When we went shopping there would be adults and children, and all our supplies, and the boat so loaded up and low in the water that the sides were only a few centimeters above the lake surface.'

'Yikes, it sounds dangerous.'

'No, not really. We usually only went when the water was calm. Although, actually, now I come to think about it, I do remember being frightened. Maybe it was only once, when I was very small and there were some waves. Maybe the wind had got up during our shopping excursion and the waves were splashing over the side of the boat. I remember that.'

'I hope you had a life-jacket.'

'No one had life-jackets in those days,' she said with a laugh. 'But listen to me, rambling on about my childhood! We should be planning your research. Where do you want to start?'

'No, no,' I said. 'This is really interesting. This is exactly what I came to Finland for, to hear what life is like here.'

'Well, it's not much like that any more. That was in the sixties, what I've been describing. Nowadays, Kelvenne is a national park and a lot more busy.'

'Okay, but imagine, Päivi, we're almost exactly the same age. If I'd been born in Finland then what you've been describing would have been my experience, too. Or something very like it. Tell me more about Kelvenne. You said there were no buildings. Was it all forest, then?'

'Yes, but not dense forest. There were some alder bushes near the shore and the central part of the island had pine trees, but they were quite far apart so it felt open. That was because of the sandy soil. The trees do not grow close together in sandy soil. Behind the beach where we camped there was an area of flat ground and then the land sloped up quite steeply to the ridge. From the top of the ridge, we could see the water on either side, and other islands dotted about, and the mainland. Between the pine trees there were bearberries, like a carpet.'

'I don't think I know bearberries.'

'They grow in sandy soil, so Kelvenne was ideal for them, and they're quite a dominant species in the right conditions, so they tend to take over ground space. That is what they had done on Kelvenne. They grow close to the ground, and very thick, and have small green leaves and a lot of deep orangey-red berries. The leaves are very dense so they form a carpet. I can still see those slopes of

50

Kelvenne in my mind, deep green, spotted with red berries everywhere. It was so beautiful.'

'I guess you collected the berries to eat, then, or are they poisonous?'

'They're not poisonous, but very bitter. We did not eat them. It is possible to, and the leaves are collected to make a kind of tea, but it's also bitter. It has medicinal properties, though. Herbalists use it to treat kidney diseases. But there were also wild strawberries on other parts of Kelvenne and we used to collect those. Oh, they were so sweet and the flavor was so intense. Nothing like the strawberries you buy in the shops. There were lots of blueberries as well, of course. You find those almost everywhere. We children used to collect them and we would earn five pennies for each full tin we collected.'

'Pennies?'

'Yes, we had marks and pennies before we got the euro. We called them *markka* and *penniä* in Finnish.'

'How about that! And I guess you ate as many of those berries as you collected.'

'Of course! They were so delicious. Although, actually, Esko used to eat much more of his than I did of mine, so I always earned more money. And I've just remembered something else. I haven't thought of this for years, but talking about those summers now to you is bringing all these memories back to my mind. We used to hang our food supplies in plastic bags from the branches of a tree to stop the horses eating it. Or was it sheep? I can't remember. But there were some farm animals that were brought to graze on the island for the summer from the farms on the mainland. It was particularly the bread, I remember, that they liked, so we had to put it high enough to be out of their reach. Other food we kept in the earth cellar.'

'Earth cellar? You were certainly well organized.'

51

'Oh yes. The men built the earth cellars by digging a hole and then making a lid with a frame of branches covered with plastic and then using a heavy stone to keep it in place. It was enough to keep birds and small animals out, but I guess the larger ones could have pushed the lid and stone off, so that's why we had to hang the bread high in the trees. Those earth cellars were surprisingly effective. We kept milk and butter in them as well as smoked and salted fish because the sheep or horses weren't so interested in those.'

'So were you the only people on the island during those summers or was it a popular thing that lots of families did?'

'I don't think we were the only people, no. But there was never anyone else within eyesight or earshot of us. We effectively had the place to ourselves. It is a long island, as you can see, and there could have been others camping further up, but we never saw them. And the lake was much quieter in those days than now. There were far fewer motorboats and none of these high speed boats that you see nowadays. It's several years since I've been to Kelvenne, but the last time I was there the atmosphere was quite different. There were constantly boats passing, and the sound of powerful engines. And there were lots of boats moored along the shore, although most of them were probably on a short visit. It's not allowed to camp there these days; the whole island is a nature reserve now.'

I'd been captivated by this account of Päivi's childhood summers and my imagination was fired by the glimpse she'd given me of this paradisiacal place and the idyllic lifestyle that her family had enjoyed there. But it was getting late. I could begin to feel the effects of my jet-lag taking hold and, more importantly, I didn't want to impose on Päivi's hospitality. It was time for me to be getting back to my hotel but before I left we discussed what the next step in my family tree and history project should be. I explained to Päivi that I'd filled in the details of the Mäkinen family from my grandfather's generation down to the present day, but that I had very little information about my grandmother's family and I thought that a good place to start would be in the parish records of Kuhmoinen. Päivi suggested that we should drive out there the next day and so we agreed that she would meet me at my hotel at ten o'clock the next morning.

Chapter Six

I didn't climb straight into bed when I got to my hotel room. Instead, I took one of the exercise books that I had with me for writing down notes of all the information I collected during my trip, and I started writing up the things that Päivi had told me that evening about her childhood summers.

I'll admit that I'd had a rather vague idea of what the contents of my family history would actually consist of. I'd imagined that I would be collecting data about my forefathers' jobs: where they lived, education, dates and places of marriages births and deaths, some description of places, and the major events of their lives. A series of mini-biographies. It sounds pretty dry and dull now. When I began writing up the story that Päivi had told me, I thought I might use some of it in the family history; an edited version would add some life and color to the section about Päivi's family.

At that stage, I recall, I imagined these events referring principally to her parents, the adult actors in the events. I must have had a strange, automatic habit of compartmentalizing the experiences of each individual, instead of seeing the full interconnectedness of their lives. I imagined the editing would involve organizing the practical arrangements for the camping trips in the parents' biographies and the memories of specific scenes or activities in Päivi's.

But I was quite wrong. It didn't happen immediately, that first evening, but within a few days, Päivi's story completely took over. I continued to collect the bare facts of names and dates for my family tree, but the story that I was writing in my notebook was Päivi's. Writing down the details that she had told me about Kelvenne was so interesting that I forgot my jet-lag and tiredness. And it raised many questions, gaps where I wanted more information to get the complete picture that I would have to ask her to fill in the next day.

By the time I finally crawled into bed I was dead beat. And as I drifted off to sleep, the images in my mind of the lake scenery, beach, and tents constructed of branches and plastic sheets were so strong and clear that I almost believed that I'd spent my childhood summers on Kelvenne myself.

I woke up at about six o'clock the next morning, feeling totally refreshed. I'd slept like a baby. The room was quite light, despite the heavy drapes, but I didn't feel as if the light had woken me. I felt like I'd had my sleep out. I reckoned that if I could stay alert through this day and sleep normally the next night, my jet-lag would be all over. I lay in bed for a while, enjoying the tranquility and the absence of demands on my time. It felt real good to be on my own.

After a while I went to look out of the window. A little traffic was already moving in the street and there were one or two pedestrians on the sidewalk. There was an early morning atmosphere, despite the fact that the sun was already quite high and the day was bright. I had my shower and was ready to go down to breakfast as soon as they started to serve it at seven o'clock.

There was no one else around as I passed along the corridor to the elevator and went down to the first floor. Even the reception desk was unmanned, temporarily, I presumed. I headed in the direction of the breakfast room. There was a hotel employee operating a large vacuum cleaner on that corridor, a young man with a swarthy complexion and black hair. He certainly didn't look like my idea of a Finn. I guessed he may have been from a Mediterranean country.

55

I was in no hurry to get my breakfast and felt in the mood for a little chat so I opened up the conversation by asking if this was the right way to the breakfast room. He assured me it was. He spoke English with quite a noticeable accent. I passed a comment on the weather and mentioned that I was from the States and then asked if he was Finnish or from abroad. It transpired that he was from Afghanistan. He'd come to Finland as an asylum seeker, he told me, some nine months earlier. I told him that my grandparents had left Finland to go to America in 1920, and then asked him how he was settling down and how he liked living in Finland. He didn't volunteer a lot of information about that, but he said that he hoped that one day he could return to his own country. I asked him how the situation was there. He talked a bit about the Russians in Afghanistan and the fighting and destruction of many buildings in his home town. Then he began to talk about the 'bad people' who took power after the Russians left. I guess he was referring to the Taliban. These were the pre-9/11 days and the Taliban hadn't achieved the high media profile that they would later, but I'd heard enough to have an idea of what my friend meant.

'Well, I hope everything works out as well for you as it did for my grandparents in America, whether you stay in Finland or go back to your own country,' I said.

At this point, I began to notice that his eyes were often looking along the corridor in the direction that I had come from, and I understood that he might be worried that his boss would come along and be annoyed if he was just standing around talking instead of getting on with his job. I didn't want to get the guy in trouble, so I wished him a good day and continued on my way to breakfast. The conversation had made me think, though, how much we have to be thankful for in the west. Most of us, at least; people like me, for example, and those lucky enough to live

56

in a safe and peaceful country like Finland. I'd never seen war, never known hunger or illness. I was confident that if I should ever become ill, there were doctors and medicines to give me the best chance possible. Thinking about that poor guy from Afghanistan, forced to leave his home, I had to acknowledge that I led a privileged existence.

There was a self-service buffet style breakfast laid out in the dining room. I checked the different bowls and dishes. There was a generous and varied selection, but not everything on offer appeared to me to be breakfast food. There was a large bowl of steaming porridge, and I thought of Päivi's comments about having to eat porridge as a child. There were cut meats and sliced cheeses and eggs, French fries, meat balls, raw fish and pickled gherkins. Well, I know that eating customs vary widely from nation to nation but I guess you can say there are two types of people in this world: those who will eat raw fish for breakfast and those who won't. I helped myself to some bread rolls, ham and a boiled egg, orange juice and a coffee and sat down to enjoy a leisurely meal.

Päivi picked me up at the hotel as agreed and we set off towards Kuhmoinen. The weather had cooled considerably since the previous day and the bright morning that I had looked out on at six o'clock had changed. There was now a lot of cloud about, although it was still dry. The sky was a pale silvery color, like the inside of an oyster shell. I had no complaints as the weather was more comfortable for sitting in a car. Päivi's didn't have air conditioning, so it was good that it wasn't too hot. But it did have a gear stick. I don't remember the last time I saw a car with manual transmission in the States.

'In Kuhmoinen we have to visit the *kirkkonherran virasto*,' Päivi began. 'That's the church registry office or parish office. I looked it up in my dictionary last night after you had left. They keep the civic records there. Everyone who has lived in the parish is registered – it's the law in Finland – and all births, deaths and marriages are recorded in the archives. For more recent dates it's not necessary to make any special arrangements, but if we later want to research back into the nineteenth century or earlier, we will have to do so.'

From Hämeenlinna we got onto a road that took us through gently rolling fields with patches of forest frequently appearing and the odd small lake. It was a peaceful and beautiful landscape, and for a while we drove in silence and I admired the view imagining what it would have been like to have lived here always. The tranquility of the scenery brought the Afghan boy (for he wasn't much more than a boy – twenty at the very most) back to my mind, and I told Päivi about him and how talking to him had made me realize how fortunate we were.

'And I came across a Russian woman working in a café in Helsinki,' I added. 'I guessed she was Russian by her accent. Now, she wouldn't have been an asylum seeker, would she? But is it possible she was an economic refugee? I really don't have much idea about the conditions of life in Russia nowadays.'

'Not an asylum seeker, certainly. There is a lot of poverty in Russia, though. Since the fall of the old Soviet Union, quite a lot of Russians have come to Finland, mainly to work and improve their standard of living, I think.'

'Like the waitress I met?'

'Could be. Many of them are from areas that were a part of Finland before the Second World War.'

'So Finland lost land to Russia then? I didn't know that.'

'Yes. That land was ceded to the Soviet Union under the peace terms. A lot of Finns got out and came west, but not all. Now some families from those areas who claim to have Finnish roots have moved to Finland. Most speak little or no Finnish, though, so they would sound like Russians. I believe that some Russian businesspeople have also started companies in Finland and some of them may employ Russian staff. They may find them cheaper. All in all, there are quite a lot of Russians living in Finland today, and I think the number's growing. There are also loads of Russian tourists. They are the rich Russians, the new rich. They come for the skiing in winter and they like the Finnish spas. That's another reason why you might meet Russian employees in restaurants and hotels. They can serve the Russian customers in their own language.'

We drove on in silence for a bit. From the map, I'd estimated that we would have at least an hour's drive to Kuhmoinen and probably closer to one and a half. I wanted to use that time to get some more information about Päivi's childhood summers on Kelvenne, so after a few minutes I brought up the subject that we'd been talking about the previous evening. I began by asking her about the journey from Lahti to Kelvenne in her uncle's boat.

'Well, we did not start exactly from Lahti,' she answered. 'Juhani's boat place was in Messilä, just outside Lahti.'

'You mean there was a marina there, or.....?'

'Yes, I suppose so, though "marina" sounds rather grand for the few wooden jetties that were there. Anyway, coming from Hämeenkoski, we took the bus to Lahti and then changed just before we got into Lahti proper and took the Hollola bus to Messilä. Imagine, with all that luggage, changing buses. I don't know how my parents managed, and with two small children, too. I was a babe in arms the first time we went, and Esko was a toddler.

'Juhani's boat was well loaded! Apart from my family there were Juhani and Raili and two of their children, Mari and Liisa. They were a little bit older than us, as you know. Panu, their eldest, was already grown up by then and he didn't come with us. But with four adults and four children, plus all the equipment, food, clothing - oh my, that boat was full.'

'And you said that you didn't have life-jackets. Wasn't it a bit dangerous with such small children on a crowded boat like that?' I asked.

'No, not really. Water was such a natural part of our environment. I'm sure we were safer there then than children are nowadays on the street.'

'Well, yes, you have a point there,' I conceded.

'I think we had different ideas about safety and danger at that time. Or maybe it was living in the country. Or maybe it was because we were children. We saw things differently. I remember in winter when I was playing with my friends, whenever we saw a snow plow - which was just a lorry with a large scoop fixed on the front - coming along the road, sending its wave of snow flying up into the air, we used to lie down at the side of the road so that the spray of snow would cover us. It was fun! But think how horrified I would be now if I saw small children lying within a meter and a half of a snow plow. Oh my God! My heart would stop.

'Anyway, on our summer trips we set off across Vesijärvi lake first, that led to Päijänne. There is a canal between the two lakes at Vääksy and I still remember how exciting it was to go into the lock and the gates closed and the water began to rush and swirl around the boat and we gradually rose up. The height difference is about three meters. And there was one funny thing: the water in Vesijärvi was green and the water in Päijänne was brown. It's to do with the nature of the land around the lakes. I always felt that when we reached the brown water, then we were on holiday. The weather conditions could change a lot, too, between the lakes. Or not exactly the weather, but the boating conditions. Päijänne is a much bigger lake and it's very long, so if the wind came from the north then the water was much rougher on the Päijänne side. Coming out of the canal and past the shelter of the first islands we sometimes came into quite big waves and Juhani's boat would roll and sway with them. I was sometimes a bit scared but Juhani was an expert boatman. He knew what he was doing.

'Some summers my other cousins joined us on Kelvenne, too. That's my father's brother, Pentti, and his wife, Raija, and their children, Petteri, Taru and Riku. I don't think they were there the first year or two, although I was too young to remember myself, of course, but that is what I've been told. But later they came as well. You will probably meet Taru while you're here. She's quite a lively character. Riku's an engineer and his work has taken him to Germany for a year, so he won't be around. I'm not sure about Petteri. They actually lived in Hämeenlinna at the time of the Kelvenne summers and they used to take the bus to Pädäsjoki, which was the closest point to Kelvenne, and Juhani took the boat there to pick them up and bring them to the island. Then we were quite a large party. There were seven of us children and we had wonderful times playing and swimming and fishing.'

'I guess you spent a lot of time in the water, right?'

'Oh yes. The beach where we always built our camp had very shallow water near the edge, ideal for small children. Then beyond the shallow water there was a thick line of reeds, then the lake bottom sloped down sharply into deep water. The men cut a channel through the reeds to bring the boat in to the beach. We always had the inner tube from a tractor, or some large vehicle. It might have been a lorry, actually. We inflated it and floated it out to the deeper water where we could clamber over it and dive from it. It was such fun for small children. And there were always some logs along the shore. They came adrift from the log rafts and washed up on Kelvenne.'

'You mean from the trees that had been cut down for timber?'

'Yes, that's right. There were often huge rafts of cut logs being towed by a tug to the sawmill. There are, or rather there were, many sawmills around the shore of Päijänne. Most of them have closed down now. Logs would sometimes come adrift and we used them as floats to play on as well. The boys would float the logs out past the reeds into the deep water and then try to stand on them, like real lumberjacks.'

Päivi stopped talking for a moment as she guided the car round a tight bend. When the road straightened out again she glanced across at me and said, 'We had a sauna there, too.'

'A sauna!' I repeated, in surprise. 'However did you manage that?'

'The men built it in the same way as they built the huts, with a frame made from branches and covered with plastic sheets. They erected it beside some rocks at the end of the beach, so that the rocks were partly inside the sauna hut. Then they hollowed out the earth and sand around and under the rocks and made a fire so that it heated the rocks. It was enough to get steam when you threw water on the hot rocks. They even made a bench to sit on in the sauna by peeling the bark from several branches and then lashing them tightly together. It was wonderful to run out of the sauna and jump into the cool lake water.'

'It's amazing,' I said. 'You seem to have thought of everything.'

'Did I tell you about our lagoons? I think I did, yesterday evening.'

'Yes, you mentioned them briefly. You said they were very deep and the water was very dark.'

'We children were captivated by them. There was something so mysterious about them. The water was always

62

dead still and flat, even on a windy day, because the banks were so high and steep and they almost surrounded the lagoon and there was a sand bank across the entrance that almost closed it off so that the waves from the lake broke there. There was a thick line of reeds along each side of the sandbank and it further helped to still the movement of the water. The reeds made a dry whispering noise in the wind that floated across the lagoons. And then they were so deep. We used to say that a monster lived in them. I pictured it as a kind of giant catfish. Or maybe it was more like a dragon, actually. One of those Chinese theater dragons. The fact that there were two lagoons right beside each other somehow doubled the mysteriousness. When there was no wind, the silence was intense. We often went there to play at the top of the slope and to watch for the monster.'

A pause followed this last comment. My imagination was full of deep, dark lagoons, still water and monsters so that I hardly noticed how the silence had lengthened until Päivi broke it.

'Poor Esko,' she added.

'Your brother,' I said. 'I noticed, of course, that he died very young, just a couple of years ago. I'm very sorry. I'd been sort of waiting for an opportunity to offer my condolences, when it would sound natural, so to speak.' Internally, I was cursing the clumsiness of this speech, which hadn't come out at all like I had wanted it to. But Päivi didn't seem to notice.

'Thank you, Len,' she said. 'Esko was something of a black sheep, you could say. As a child he was very lively. Too lively, perhaps, or what's called hyperactive, I think. He was one of those children who is always having accidents and hurting themselves and it was partly because he took everything at a rush. Always racing on his bike, usually down the steepest hill he could find, without thinking what might be at the bottom of it. He was the same on skis. When the boys played dares, he was always the one who would do the thing that no one else would. He always had to be the one to climb highest up a tree and then couldn't get down. He didn't seem to have any fear and it was largely because he didn't give any thought to possible consequences. He was the same when he grew up. First it was cars. He drove much too fast. He had several accidents and one was quite serious. Oh well,' and she gave a deep sigh as a sign of moving on.

'Skiing,' she suddenly burst out. 'I haven't told you about my skiing days, have I?'

'No,' I replied, 'but I'd sure love to hear about them.'

I was still wondering about Esko. Päivi hadn't said how he had died and I didn't ask. Her mention of skiing seemed very much like changing the subject so I guessed she wouldn't appreciate being pressed on the topic. I had an idea that I would hear the rest of that part of the story later, and I was right.

'I've been skiing for as long as I can remember,' she began. 'My father was a very keen and active member of the local skiing club and both Esko and I learned to ski at the same time as we started to walk. Right from when we were very small there were little competitions; at primary school, at first. Later I joined the skiing club and went to local competitions. I was quite good. I often won those small races. Then when I was about thirteen, there was a shortage of women for the senior team so I started skiing with them. I didn't win against the best adult women in the area, but I did quite well. And in my own age group I won the regional championship several times. I did well in the national championship, too. My best place was ninth.'

'Wow!' I said. 'You must have been real good. So were you in the national team? Have you ever skied for Finland?'

'No. That would have been the next step, I suppose. I was fifteen when I came ninth in the national and I went to a couple of national training camps after that. The next winter I would probably have gone to some national level competitions, but you can probably guess what happened.'

'Did you get an injury, then?' I asked.

Päivi laughed. 'No,' she said, 'I discovered boys and discos. And cigarettes, though I gave those up years ago, I'm glad to say.'

It was on the tip of my tongue to ask, *What about the boys and discos?* but I didn't dare to be so familiar. I was quite sure she would have taken it as a joke. But I hesitated so long that it wouldn't have sounded sufficiently spontaneous and so I missed the opportunity.

We were arriving on the edge of Kuhmoinen by now and as we drove through the outskirts Päivi started looking out for turnings and street names, which put an end to her skiing reminiscences for then and I had to wait until later to hear further details about that part of her life.

Chapter Seven

Kuhmoinen is a sleepy little village set in the middle of a forest and lake landscape at the end of a long creek off Lake Päijänne. Päivi parked the car outside the town office building and we went inside to find the church registry office, as she called it. Päivi led the search for the Virtanens of my grandmother's family, explaining and translating to me the information she was turning up. It wasn't hard to make progress. We found many details of my grandmother's parents and her brothers and sisters which I added to that side of my family tree. We also found dates of marriages and some births but when we tried to trace the course of the next generation, we found that all of them had left the parish early in their adult lives.

'That is maybe going to cause some problems,' Päivi said, 'because Virtanen is the most common surname in Finland. It will be difficult to trace those who went to larger towns, which appears to be most of them. They probably left Kuhmoinen to look for work. However, there is this one son, Joosepi, who moved to Kuhmalahti. That's a fairly small village and it's quite close to Kuhmoinen. Joosepi was twenty-four when he left here, so it's quite possible that he went to that new village to get married. It's close enough that he could have been courting a girl from there. We could visit Kuhmalahti later to see if a Joosepi Virtanen got married there around the same time.'

Päivi asked the clerk how far back the records went and he told her that the earlier parish records had been destroyed in a fire. It was only possible to trace back as far as my grandmother's grandparents, and the same on my grandfather's side.

I was very glad to get so much new information, but all the time I couldn't help thinking about Päivi's history. I felt impatient to know more about the skiing club and competitions that she had begun describing. It was kind of frustrating to have to direct my attention to this surveying of the old parish records when I would honestly much rather have been listening to Päivi's story. However, I was genuinely keen to make my family tree as complete as possible. I was also very keen to see the places where they had lived. We noted down the addresses in the records and Päivi asked the clerk for directions to these places. There were a couple of houses near the center of Kuhmoinen and the farm where my grandmother had grown up, the one I remembered from photographs, I presumed. We also found the location of my grandfather's family's home.

Because the house addresses were so close we visited them first, but the buildings on those plots were of more recent construction and the families who occupied them were not Virtanens or Mäkinens. Still, it gave me a strange feeling to know that my grandmother's brothers and sisters, and her nieces and nephews, would have walked along the streets and paths that I was now walking myself; and in another part of the village that my grandfather's family had walked along those streets.

I tried to recall them as clearly as I could from my childhood, tried to bring back specific scenes and occasions when I'd been with them. I tried to imagine how the locations and scenes in Kuhmoinen would have been so vivid in their minds then, as if I'd been able to read those recollections that they had stored in their memories. I imagined planting the knowledge into their minds, and into my own as I was then, that I would one day stand in their home village and walk where they had grown up. As if we had been able, back then, to read this future that I was now living. Rather fanciful ideas, I know, but they seemed to encapsulate, for me, an awareness of the strangeness of the passage of time and the generations.

In fact, of course, the village was nothing like it would have looked when they left. Most of the buildings in the center were of much more recent date and so were many of the residential buildings scattered around. But still the layout of the place and the streets may have been on the same plan as when they lived here, and the natural surroundings would not have changed much.

That left my grandmother's parents' farm, which I was even keener to see. I'd told Päivi, of course, about the photos I remembered my grandmother showing me and how I believed that they must have been of this farm we were about to visit. I was real anxious to see that place. Before we started the short drive, though, to where the clerk had indicated it was located, we stopped for lunch in a simple restaurant in the center of Kuhmoinen. I told Päivi how much I appreciated her generosity with her time and help. She replied that, actually, she was glad to have something to do.

'I would only be sitting around at home or sitting in Mum's flat while she watched television,' she added. 'Some of my non-teaching friends are still at work in the week. And those who are on holiday are traveling. So it's actually very nice for me to have something to occupy my time. I just hope that I'm not forcing my company on you.'

'Good heavens, no,' I replied. 'The very idea is quite unthinkable.'

'Well, as soon as you want some time on your own to go off and do men's things, just tell me.'

'Erm…What exactly do you mean by "men's things"?' I asked, rather nervously.

'Oh, I don't know: hunting, fishing, wrestling with the bears.'

'I'm not that macho type,' I said, laughing.

'Do you like fishing?'

'Oh, from time to time,' I answered.

'We could organize a day's fishing on the lake, if you want.'

'Sure, that sounds nice.'

Our meals arrived and, as we started to eat, I directed the conversation back to the subject I was most interested in.

'So tell me more about your skiing days.'

'I spent hours training,' Päivi replied. 'In the winter I skied nearly every day and in the summers I had a training programme that included running, swimming and different kinds of exercises. I used to sort of jog up a steep hill using the ski sticks to push myself up. Many times, up and down. That was to develop the arm muscles. My father planned all my training schedule and he always came with me to competitions. He took care of my skis for me, waxing them and so on. Sports in general, and particularly skiing, were his passion. He was secretary of our club and usually acted as an official at the skiing competitions. It really took up a lot of his time. He was so pleased that I was keen on it, and he was very disappointed when I gave it up, too. We had some rows at that time, as you can probably imagine. I think it was his dream that I would reach international level and, just as I was getting close, I lost all my enthusiasm for it.

'But when I was younger, skiing was my whole life and I did train very hard. Father planned my diet as well, so that I got the right kind of nutrition, but I trained so hard that I think I used more energy than I was eating. That's why I'm so small now,' she said, smiling.

'We were always together, my father and me. He devoted a lot of time to the club and my training. I didn't think about it then − I was just a kid − but in a way he did rather neglect Esko and my mum. She's a bit weak-willed, my mum, she tends to accept everything and say nothing, but when I look back now I realize that she was not very happy about the way father was always away from home with me.

Sports and my skiing always came first. Since father died, we've talked a little bit about those days and she has hinted in a rather roundabout fashion that she felt that he never considered what she wanted to do. He just decided everything and she was expected to go along with it.'

'But what about Esko?' I asked. 'Wasn't he interested in skiing, too?'

'Not in the same way. He did ski, of course. He was quite a typical boy and liked playing several sports. He was always on the go: what they call hyperactive these days. But he did not have the kind of determination that I had. He never could stick at anything. Poor Esko. He liked ski jumping more than skiing. And he played football in the summer. Ski jumping suited his temperament more. Each jump lasts just a few seconds. That suited Esko's attention span. He was quite fearless, which is kind of a good thing in a ski jumper, but with Esko it meant he was always having accidents, falling and hurting himself. I guess he was quite good at ski jumping. He belonged to the club and he took part in some local competitions. But he was never a winner. He did not have the commitment.'

She seemed to be thinking for a few seconds and then went on.

'It's very sad, really, the way things went with Esko. You don't mind me going on like this, do you Len?' she suddenly asked. 'I do not want to bore you with all my reminiscences.'

'Päivi, absolutely not,' I insisted. 'I'm fascinated. I want to hear all about your life and experiences. I feel that I'm really getting to know you, and that's what I came to Finland for, to learn who my Finnish relatives are.'

'This is the part where I might start to get a bit melancholy.'

'Päivi, seriously, I'm very interested, but I also don't want to pry or to upset you. I hope you don't feel that you

70

have to talk about anything that is painful, or that you'd rather forget, just to satisfy my curiosity.'

'Oh no, it's not like that, Len. In a way, I want to talk about it. I have a feeling that *not* talking about things has been a rather bad habit in my family. You see, the truth is that my father did neglect Esko and my mum to do all his sporting activities and to support mine. I'm sure he did not realise it himself at the time. In fact, I'm sure that he felt he was doing a good thing to spend so much time with me, felt that he was being a good father. But I also realized later, when I was an adult, that Esko was upset about it.

He was a child, too, of course, and I do not believe that he could have articulated or explained his feelings. But I'm pretty sure that he felt left out and he resented it. I think it may well have also undermined his self-confidence, so that he believed himself to be not as good as others. That feeling would have started when he compared how our father treated him and me. I guess he would have attributed the different treatment to the fact that I was successful and that he did not get a share of the attention because he was not successful. I believe that is the conclusion he drew.

'When he grew up he could never settle or stick at anything. It's as if he always expected to fail. He trained as a car mechanic and I think he was quite good at it, but he could never keep a job. And alcohol was a problem right from his teens. Alcohol was the immediate reason why he lost jobs and became so unreliable. I used to get drunken phone calls from him in the middle of the night at one stage. Then I managed to speak to him once when he was sober and told him quite straight that he had to stop that. And he did. There was a reasonable person inside him somewhere. And he was always in debt and borrowing money. The bailiff came to his home several times, though I cannot believe he found much to take away. Esko would

71

have found that a huge joke,' Päivi said, with a short, humorless laugh.'

'Poor guy. It sure sounds like he didn't have things easy.'

'Alcohol ruined any relationships he had with women,' Päivi continued. 'At one stage there was a woman that he was serious about. They lived together for a year or more, but Esko was impossible, I'm afraid. He developed into an alcoholic and that's what killed him. The direct cause was a heart attack, but the heart attack was due to alcoholism. He started to get epileptic attacks, too, when he was in his thirties, and that was also the result of drinking.

'Father realized too late what the problem was, what he had done. He never talked about it. That wasn't his way. Keep things bottled up inside and don't show what you're feeling, was much more his style. But I could see that he was very tolerant of Esko's behavior, more so than he would otherwise have been. He tried to smooth his way as much as he could. I know he paid several of Esko's more serious debts. I'm sure he felt guilty and partly responsible for many of Esko's troubles.

'It's all very sad. And it must have made him feel worse that I had given up the skiing anyway. In a sense, the neglect and sacrifice of the family was all for nothing. I don't mean that it would have justified it if I had continued with the skiing, only that it put a spotlight on his mistake when I gave it up anyway. I'm afraid he was a disappointed man at the end of his life, my father. And it does trouble me, Len. That's why it's good to have someone to talk to about it. It's very difficult to talk to my relatives like this. It would be impossible with my mum to be as direct as this. You Americans are much better at getting problems out in the open.'

Her expression had been serious and doleful as she recounted these sad details. I'd been prepared for tears, as a matter of fact. But the last sentence was accompanied by a glance straight to my eyes and a smile like the sun coming out after a day of grey clouds. I know that sounds like a dreadful cliché, but it describes the brightening of her expression so well. Perhaps the reason we have clichés at all is precisely that they are so accurate.

'I want you to know how much I feel for you in this sorrow, Päivi,' I started. 'We all make mistakes and some of them have lasting and devastating consequences. We learn and understand things too late. But I also believe that it's human nature to find joy and happiness where we can, almost no matter what the circumstances. I'm sure both Esko and your father had many moments of real pleasure and contentment, even alongside the pain and regrets.'

'Thank you, Len. That was a very beautiful thought. And I'm sure you're right. There's still one more thing I haven't told you, though. When Esko was a toddler, the first summer that we went to Kelvenne, he fell into the water. I don't remember, of course, I was only a few months old, but it was sometimes mentioned when I was a child. He almost drowned, but mum found him in time and he was okay. That's the story as it was told to me but I have often wondered how long he was under the water and whether the lack of oxygen to the brain could have caused some brain damage. It might explain his hyperactive behavior and lack of concentration. It might also have had an influence on the epileptic attacks. Of course, it's equally possible that those things were in his genes. You just don't know, do you?'

These sadder elements in Päivi's story cast something of a shadow over what I had previously perceived as some kind of idyll, almost a lost Eden. I realized that I'd been simplifying and idealizing to no small degree. Of course, life here was not radically different to any other place on earth, at least regarding the terms on which it is lived.

We left the restaurant and drove out of Kuhmoinen, following the directions the parish clerk had given us. The route took us through forested country first, then down a narrow side-road through fields, past a small lake and eventually to a gravel track with overgrown fields and bushes, bordered by forest. I could see that this land had not been worked for years.

Sure enough, when we arrived at the location of the farm, there was very little sign left of the farm buildings. There was nothing more of the main building than the foundation stones on which the wooden structure would have rested. There was a grassed area at the front and sides of the site and several very overgrown berry bushes around its edges. It was possible to make out where paths would have led to the front and back doors and out towards the fields, and to see where the outbuildings would have been. We wandered along these half-obliterated paths and it gave me a strange feeling to know that my grandmother's feet would have stepped on this very ground, helping to wear the track that mine were now following. My grandmother's feet, and her parents' feet, and their parents' before them.

There were some rotting timbers and other materials lying around in the overgrown grass but most of the structures had been cleared away, the materials collected to use in other buildings, Päivi reckoned.

It was a disappointment, in some ways, though I'd been prepared for it. But we walked away from the site of the buildings and onto the land where the fields had been and I stood where my forefathers had ploughed, sown and harvested. They would have cleared this land that was gradually returning back to nature, too, probably as far as the line of trees where the forest began. I looked towards the trees, seeing the same view that they would have looked on as they worked. From the trees some bird that I couldn't identify was calling. Very faintly, another bird

74

replied, like an echo. I thought of the painting by Ellen Thesleff and the dead generations that had handled those wooden farm implements. I tried to imagine how it would feel for me to call this place home.

Chapter Eight

Soon after leaving Kuhmoinen on our way back to Hämeenlinna, we came to a place where Päivi said that there was a traditional old Finnish farmhouse which was now a museum.

'Would you like to stop and see it?' she asked. 'It's probably something like the kind of place your grandmother would have lived in.'

'You bet,' I replied enthusiastically.

Päivi turned off the main road and drove down a dirt track for a mile or so until we came to an open area of grass before a fairly large, old wooden building. She parked the car there and we went into the museum. The farm buildings were about a hundred and fifty years old and laid out in a simple design: the main farmhouse, outbuildings, barn and storehouses arranged in a rectangle around a grass courtyard. The farmhouse was painted a rusty reddish-brown, most of the other buildings were unpainted, and the wood was grey with age.

We went into the main building first. The whole structure stood on several large blocks of stone that lifted it above the ground, as I had seen at the site of my grandmother's farm. It was constructed with one large room which occupied about half of the building. A largish kitchen opened off the main room and there were three smaller rooms at the other end. Right in the centre of the structure was a large brick chimney that formed part of the wall between the main room and kitchen. At the base of the chimney there was an enclosed fireplace and oven also constructed of brick.

'This is very typical of farmhouses from this period, ' Päivi said, as we stood in front of the fireplace. 'These fireplaces were constructed so that the heat circulated

76

through channels in the brickwork, heating the whole structure which would then store the heat and radiate it for many hours. In the winter the fire would be alight all day, of course, and the brickwork would stay warm through the night. You see that platform area above the fireplace, to one side of the chimney? Well, that's where people would sleep in winter. They got the warmth from the chimney all night. Even when the temperature is minus twenty degrees centigrade and there is no other heating, that place stays really warm all night. When I was small I stayed in old farmhouses sometimes and I've slept on those – *pankkoouuni*, they're called, I guess there's no word in English – and it's lovely and cozy and warm.'

'It sounds great.'

We walked through the building, then went outside and admired the wooden shingle roof. I thought of the story I remembered my grandfather telling me of the men cutting the shingles and making a roof like that. We looked into the tiny wooden huts where the farmhands would have slept and the storerooms where there were various original farm implements, all made of wood and simple metalwork.

'But how did they manage in these huts in the winter?' I asked as we peered into the tiny sleeping space. There wasn't any kind of fireplace or method of heating it that I could see.

'They didn't,' Päivi replied. 'These huts would only have been used in the summers when the farm hired extra, temporary staff for the period when there was more work.'

'So then where did the workers go? When the summer work was finished?'

'Back to their family homes in most cases. If they were lucky they got some other work, or some family members had work. If they were unlucky, they went hungry.'

Finally, we went into the sauna building. It was quite cramped and rather dim, despite the bright light outside.

77

There was no window at all in the hot room and only a small one in the dressing room.

'Can you imagine how it would feel in the hot room, in winter, when it's dark outside and deep in snow and the only light comes from a candle or two on the floor near the door? And outside it's minus ten or twenty degrees centigrade and inside you're sweating and throwing water on the hot stones and the steam feels hot on your skin?'

'It must be lovely,' I said.

Päivi laughed. 'You don't sound very sure. A hundred years ago, babies were born in the sauna.'

'That must have been hot work,' I answered, without thinking.

Päivi laughed again. 'The sauna was not hot. They used it for childbirth because it was sterile and there was hot water in here. In the winter, of course, they would have had a small fire in the stove. It was easy to keep warm because it's such a small area. Plenty of older people today were born in the sauna. Juho was.'

One of the outbuildings was used as a small cafeteria and there were three tables outside, on the edge of the courtyard. When we'd finished looking round the buildings, we bought two cups of coffee and sat at one of the tables.

'When I was at school I had a friend, Ulla, who lived in a farmhouse quite similar to this. I often went to stay with her. That was one of the farmhouses where I slept on the pankkouuni in winter. It was a lovely old place, built on gently rising ground close to a large lake.'

'Would that have been Lake Päijänne?'

'No, not Päijänne, a different lake. The lake shore was about four hundred meters from the house and there was a small sandy beach where we went to play and swim in the summer. There was a shallow bay, fringed with bulrushes at one end of the beach. The water was perfectly clear and we used to climb up onto a rock, or onto a branch of a tree,

78

and we could see down to the sandy lake bottom several meters out from the shore. It was such a beautiful spot. There were clumps of water lilies with vivid yellow flowers and spiky petals, and other kinds of water plants and weeds, and in the open water between them we could see the fish moving about. It was easy to identify the different species: the roach, with a dab of red on their fins, the striped sides of perch, a small pike hanging motionless below a lily pad.

'Did you have a favourite kind of fish?'

'I particularly liked watching the bream. They were quite big fish and sometimes a shoal of them would swim across the bay, sucking up the silt and blowing it out in a yellow ochre cloud. We could see it all quite clearly. They swam slowly, if you did not scare them, as if they were tired or lazy. I always imagined them as tired old men. We used to spend hours watching the water life and the patterns of the sunlight moving with the ripples. It was quite hypnotic. Sometimes there would be a heavy splash in the reeds as a larger pike took one of the smaller fish.'

'I guess you know the names of most of the fish and animals and plants.'

'Quite a few, yes. I think I know all the fish and animals, and most of the birds but I do not know all the forest plants. Although I do know a lot of them because we all had to make a collection of dried plants when we were at primary school and stick them in a scrapbook. Mum's probably still got it somewhere.'

I thought to myself how interesting it would be to turn the pages of Päivi's schoolwork. While I was imagining that, Päivi had obviously got lost in the past for moment. The silence drew my attention back to her, and as I glanced at her eyes they lost their faraway look and focused on mine.

'Behind their farmhouse,' she continued, 'the ground sloped up more steeply, through some forest, to a ridge which had several outcrops of bare rock along its back. There was a wonderful view from those open places. You could see all the surrounding country, the dense forest beyond the fields with all its different shades of green depending on the type of trees - birch, pine, fir, spruce, maple and even the odd oak. And the lakes looked like blue silk when the sun was behind you, or like glass when you were looking towards the sun, as if half the landscape had been glazed.'

'You make it sound really wonderful.'

'It was. I remember that when I looked at the land spread out like that at my feet, I used to feel as if I was a giant and could step across from the ridge to the opposite shore of the lake in one stride. I loved that feeling,' she added, almost wistfully.

'How old were you when you visited that farm?' I asked.

'I knew Ulla when I was in middle school, so from eleven to sixteen. We lost touch a bit when I went to high school and she went to vocational school. Actually, I went to stay with her more at the beginning, at eleven, twelve, thirteen. We'd already started to drift apart before the end of middle school.

'Ulla had a younger brother and sister and we all four used to take picnics up to the ridge and tell each other ghost stories. Ulla was really great at telling them. It seemed like almost every house in her village was haunted.

'Ulla's dad was a carpenter, not a farmer, but they had some land as well. There was a field of potatoes that I used to help collect in the autumn. I did that several years. There was a meadow beside their house which may also have belonged to them. I don't know. I didn't really think about ownership at the time. It was just land. I used to help with

80

the haymaking in that meadow but I cannot remember what happened to the hay.

'They used to put up a tent in a corner of that meadow – a real tent, made of canvas – and leave it there for most of the summer. I didn't stay the whole summer, though. I would usually stay there for a few days at a time, maybe a week in the summer.'

'So this was at a later time than your summers on Kelvenne?'

'Yes. I stopped going to Kelvenne when I was about ten, but my family kept going for a few more summers. I sometimes joined them later, with my grandparents or aunt and uncle, if they were going.

'That canvas tent seemed like the height of sophistication after our self-made huts on Kelvenne. We used the tent for shelter if there was a shower when we were out playing. Sometimes we slept the night in it. There were large patches of wild mint that grew along the border of the meadow and the smell of mint was strong inside the tent, especially after rain. There were always lots of butterflies, too, and we used to feed the sparrows that would hop right under the tent flaps for crumbs from our sandwiches.'

'We used to play games in which we pretended to be pioneers in the Wild West and the tent was our homestead being attacked by red Indians. Or sometimes it was a fort. We even built a crude platform in a tree beside the tent – oh, okay, it was Ulla's dad who built it – and we used to climb up there to look out for the enemy. We called it the guard's roost. I suppose Ulla and I were getting a bit old for those kinds of childish games but her little brother and sister liked it so we played along, too. And it was fun. Actually, it was like deliberately delaying the end of childhood, knowingly being more childish than we really were. Knowingly innocent; that's a nice idea, isn't it?'

'It sounds like you had an idyllic childhood, Päivi. I don't remember anything as exciting as a genuine tree house in my childhood. I guess you could say I was kind of innocent, but not deliberately so. A late developer, you could call me.'

'I still remember one of the stories that Ulla told us one day when we were sheltering in the tent with the rain pattering on the taut canvas. It was about a very big snake that one farm worker found. There were quite a lot of real snakes in the area, actually. But in the story, this snake was much bigger than usual, longer than the farm worker's arm and almost as thick. It had coiled up and gone to sleep in one of the stacks of grass that were set up to dry at haymaking. He tried to kill it but the snake was too fast and kept dodging the man's blows, and then suddenly the snake reared up its head and bit the man on his tongue and where it bit him there were two holes that began to bleed. But the blood turned to fire so flames were flying out of his mouth and all around him there was the newly dried hay so of course it immediately caught fire and the whole meadow went up in flames, whoosh, and all the hay was lost.'

Päivi told the story with great animation and expression, getting faster and quite breathless as she reached the climax and bursting into laughter when it was finished.

'Wow, what an amazing story,' I said. 'You told it really well.'

'It *is* quite a story, isn't it? I don't know where Ulla got them all from. I think she made them up herself. She always had stories like that.' She paused and frowned slightly. 'At least, I think it was one of Ulla's. Or did I hear it somewhere else? Silly, I can't really remember now. It's just that when I remembered the story, I had the smell of the wild mint so strongly in my mind that I thought it must have come from that time. Oh well, it doesn't really matter. I expect it probably was Ulla's.'

After leaving the farmhouse museum, we continued on our way to Hämeenlinna, passing through the village of Padasjoki. Päivi mentioned that Aino had a small summer cottage near the village. She said that it would be possible to spend a couple of days there, if I wanted. 'It's right on the lake,' she added. 'A very beautiful spot, though the cottage itself is very basic. But it does have electricity, at least.'

'I'd love to,' I replied.

'And Aino is very keen to meet you. And Juho, too. Would you like to visit them tomorrow? Or do you have any other plans?'

'I don't have any plans,' I answered. 'It would be great to meet them. I'm especially looking forward to meeting Juho because he was born before my grandparents left Finland. In a sort of way, he's the last living link to that life that they left behind.'

'He was in touch with your grandparents until they died, as you know, and may still have some of the letters that they sent. The last time I spoke to him, I mentioned it and he said he would have a look to see if he could find any.'

So the following day I went with Päivi to visit Aino and then we all went to Juho's apartment. They both lived alone as Juho's wife, Eila, had died in 1988 and Aino was unmarried. She was a fairly quiet woman but I got the impression that nothing much escaped her attention. She was always alert. She could say a few words in English and I appreciated that she did her best to be welcoming to me and to make me feel at home, but most of the time she spoke Finnish and Päivi translated for me.

Juho was over eighty at that time but in very good health. He was quieter than Aino. He didn't say very much at all, really, but he had a very warm smile and small twinkling eyes that seemed to nearly disappear into the folds and wrinkles of his skin. Several times, when I

83

glanced towards him, I noticed that he was watching me quite intensely with that almost mischievous smile. I wondered what he was thinking. He couldn't have been looking for my grandparents' features in me because he'd never actually met them, unless, perhaps, when he was a baby, which he wouldn't have remembered, of course. Maybe he could see some resemblance to his own mother's features. She was my grandfather's sister, after all.

Juho had managed to find some of the letters that my grandparents had sent him and handed them to Päivi who read through and translated several passages to me. There was a letter announcing my own birth amongst them, which gave me a strange feeling. I took the letter in my hands and looked at the lines and shapes that were quite indecipherable to me and which represented what would have been the sounds of my native tongue if my grandparents hadn't emigrated. There was a sentence telling what name my parents planned to give me. That was the only word I could have read and it was spelled 'Lennart'.

After we'd left I mentioned to Päivi that Juho had seemed to find something interesting in my face.

'He usually watches and listens like that,' she said. 'He's a bit of a silent Finn, much as I dislike and disagree with that stereotype, but Juho does rather conform to the image. He's really very jolly, though, and he's got this ironic sense of humor.'

'He has an engaging smile. I felt very sympathetic towards him. I wondered if he was seeing some familiar Mäkinen characteristic in me?'

Päivi stopped and looked closely into my face until I began to feel slightly self conscious. 'There's not really anything that I can identify,' she concluded. 'Perhaps he was thinking about something else.'

Chapter Nine

The day after we had visited Aino and Juho, I arranged to go on a lake sightseeing cruise. That was partly so that I could give Päivi a break from being my guide, but also because I was keen to see the lake scenery. There was a company in Lahti that offered various excursions that took different routes. Päivi had sent me details about these trips along with other information for tourists when I was planning my visit to Finland. I'd chosen a trip that covered part of the south end of Lake Päijänne and which included a commentary on the influences of the ice age on the geography of the area. The commentary was given in English and German as well as Finnish and I reckoned that this would add an interesting dimension to the cruise. It would also take me through the Vääksy canal with the lock that Päivi had told me about when she described the trip from Lahti to Kelvenne.

It was easy to get from Hämeenlinna to Lahti by bus in time to join the cruise. Päivi had offered to drive me, as I'd guessed she would, but I told her that I simply wouldn't allow her to be my chauffeur to that extent.

I'd come to realize after the first research trip to Kuhmoinen that my original plan was not going to work out quite as I'd pictured it. Actually, I hadn't really pictured it very clearly at all, nor thought about what would be involved in extensive research into the family tree. It was obvious to me now, though, that it would mean asking an awful lot of Päivi because of my dependence on her Finnish and although I felt that she would probably insist, as she had already done, that she was happy to offer her assistance, I began to feel too embarrassed to keep asking for so much. This was part of the reason for me adjusting my goals.

Another factor was that I did now have some details from my grandmother's family and, although that side wasn't complete, I was satisfied. I'd seen the places where my forebears had lived, too. That was something that had been important to me and now I felt that I'd filled that gap in my sense of myself. And finally, I was beginning to realize, at a more conscious level now, that Päivi's story was taking over and starting to dominate my thoughts. I'd continued to make notes of all that she'd told me. I thought that I might extend these notes to include a similar record of Aino's and Juho's lives, if the details came my way. Or of other relatives that I might still meet. I decided to play it by ear and just wait to see what turned up.

So I was very pleased when, the day after my lake cruise, Päivi told me that Aino had suggested that the three of us should spend a few days at her cottage near Padasjoki. That would give us plenty of time to talk and reminisce and quite likely I would learn further facts about their lives. They'd been in contact with some of Päivi's cousins and Aino's aunt Liisa, who was actually younger than Aino and only three years older than Päivi. Liisa and Taru would both come to the cottage while we were staying there so I'd be able to meet them, too.

'Liisa is Juhani's daughter,' Päivi added. 'He was the youngest of your grandfather's siblings, by quite many years, as you probably remember, and they got Liisa quite late in life. Liisa was what we call an evening star in Finnish, meaning a baby born when the parents are already getting towards middle age.'

Aino's cottage was, as Päivi had said, basic. What we would call a shack in Minnesota. It was a simple, wooden structure, with a veranda along the side that faced the lake. A door from the veranda opened directly into the living room which had a small kitchen area in the corner and two doors on the right that led to two small bedrooms. There was a sauna behind the bedroom walls with a separate entrance from the veranda, and a separate sauna in a small wooden building down by the lake shore.

'Two saunas?' I said, questioningly.

'Yes, the beach sauna is a more recent addition. Aino uses mainly the beach sauna in the summers because it's close to the water, and the cottage sauna in the autumn because it provides heat through the wall to the bedrooms, which you would not want in the summer, of course.'

There was no running water in the cottage. We had to fetch drinking water from a well in the corner of the plot. Water for washing could be drawn from the lake by a hand pump in the cottage sauna or carried by bucket from the lake to the beach sauna. Both sauna stoves had a large tank that could be filled with lake water and heated, actually to boiling point, when the sauna was in use. The beach sauna was heated every evening while I was there. The water was still quite warm the following morning. The cottage had electricity and there was a refrigerator and a gas cooker with the gas supplied from a cylinder. An open fireplace provided warmth on chilly evenings and during the fall, when the cottage was still in use.

It wasn't possible to stay there during the winter, though, Päivi said, because the insulation was not sufficient. It looked as though the cottage had been furnished with old furniture that had become so shabby that it had to be replaced in the town dwelling but was taken into use in the cottage. 'Shabby' doesn't sound very complimentary, I know, but it describes the chairs and sofa accurately. I should add that the whole place was very cozy and comfortable. A small fiberglass rowing boat was pulled up on the shore and there was a five horsepower outboard motor in the shed, enough to make short trips on the lake.

And the location was stunning. The plot was wooded, but the area in front of the cottage was clear down to the lake shore. There was a small bay and beyond it the open water with a couple of small islands and, beyond them, what I took to be the opposite shore at first but which was actually another, much larger island that turned out to be Kelvenne. The shoreline was densely wooded, with here and there other small cottages amongst the trees.

When we arrived, in the early afternoon, the air was still, the sky was unbroken pale grey cloud, and the lake like a mirror reflecting the trees and cloud. The world seemed to have turned to silver and grey. It was astonishingly beautiful and peaceful. There is scenery like that in Minnesota, too, and I had driven through part of it many times. Most of my sightseeing had been done from a car. I'm a city boy through-and-through. The countryside looks good to me through glass but I'd never been much interested in walking through it. I didn't do any serious hiking in Finland, nothing like, but I somehow felt that I had gotten closer to nature there.

'You're getting to see the area quite well,' Päivi said after we had settled in. 'What with your lake cruise and Kuhmoinen and now this Padasjoki shore, you will have quite a clear picture of the places your grandparents would have known.'

'It's all been really fantastic,' I replied.

'We can take the boat to Kelvenne while we're here, it's not far. I can show you the place where we used to camp.'

'Now that, I would really like.'

'You know, Len, telling you all about my childhood days has set me thinking more about some of those events. I was talking with my mum the day that you were on the cruise and I asked her about some of the details that I could not remember so clearly. And gradually I worked round to the topic of Esko falling in the water. I didn't want to upset her so I didn't ask directly what had happened but we talked in general about those Kelvenne

88

summers for a bit, about the practical arrangements and food and cooking, and which years my other cousins came and so on. At last I got to the point where I could mention Esko's accident as a natural progression of the subject and she described what she remembered.'

I could sense the slight tension in Päivi's voice. I felt as if the world had gone suddenly silent, but I think it was just because I was focused so intently on what she would say next.

'It was quite strange. She told it as if it was a joke, like a funny anecdote. She said that she had been fishing and that was why she had not noticed what he was doing or where he was, because she was concentrating on her float. And then she realized he was gone and she started looking and found him floating face down, spreadeagled. She told the story with unusual gusto, unusual for her – she's generally quite inexpressive. It was very weird to listen to. I've been trying to understand what she was thinking and feeling. I mean, at the time it happened, she must have been in an awful panic and when she first saw him like that she must have wondered if he was dead or alive.

'And when she got him out of the water and he recovered, it must have been a massive relief. I can only think that her attitude to the incident now is the effect of that mixture of guilt and relief. I guess she's sort of denying the responsibility, subconsciously I mean.

'It was clear as we spoke that she didn't have any idea how long Esko had been in the water. How could she let a toddler play near deep water like that without watching him? It seems so incredibly irresponsible. To be just concentrating on fishing while a toddler under two years of age is running around. She actually said that she'd gone to a place where the water was deep because it was good for fishing and she took Esko with her.'

'Of course, it may only have been a matter of seconds that he was in the water,' I said. 'Her instincts may have warned her almost immediately that he wasn't around.'

'Yes, it's possible. It upset me to hear her talking like that, actually. I didn't say anything to her. I didn't want to make her feel guilty now, after all this time. I'm sure it must have been an awful shock when it happened. I guess it must be some kind of denial.'

'It sounds like a very horrible experience,' I said. 'I think you were probably right not to probe into it any deeper with your mother.'

'She's a funny case, my mum. It can be quite frustrating to be around her. In some ways I feel sorry for her and at other times I get quite annoyed and have to bite my tongue to keep from saying something sharp.'

'Well, I think that's not an unusual feeling.'

'No, maybe not. She's very dependent, you know, and all her life she has always had someone to make decisions for her and tell her what to do. She went straight from her parents' home to being a wife. I mean, she never lived independently as a single woman. Well, of course that was the usual way in those days. A lot of women lived with their parents until they got married. And my mum was very young when she got married, under twenty, in fact, and she got her first baby very soon. That was Maarit, my sister that I never knew. She only lived for a few months. It must have been very hard for my mum, and father too, of course. From time to time over the years, they both talked a little about the loss of their first baby. From what they said, I worked out that my mother was depressed for some time afterwards, but there was little understanding of depression in those days. She had to cope by herself. Poor old mum. She hasn't had an easy life.

'Her mother, my grandmother, was a very strong personality, and then my father was rather dominant, so my mother has always been led by more forceful personalities. Now that she's on her own, she can't make decisions for herself. She's always asking me what she should do, or how to manage her affairs. It can be quite comic sometimes but it can be dreadfully irritating, too. Do you know, I've sometimes offered her a chocolate from a box where they are all the same and she can't decide which one to take.' Päivi sighed and shook her head slightly. 'Is it horrible of me to talk like this about my own mother?'

'No, of course not, ' I replied. 'These little frictions and tensions are perfectly natural. They don't mean anything bad.'

'That's good to hear. And she's not as bad as I make out when I'm annoyed with her. In many ways I feel a bit sorry for her. Yeah, she's always been led by stronger personalities, and she's never had a chance to use her own talents. She's actually very clever with her hands. She can make anything in the way of clothes, knitwear or stuffed soft toys, and she's quite good at drawing. But she never had any training and she's never had a job using her skills. It's a shame.

'I don't take after her. I'm more like my grandmother. I've always been very independent and determined, even as a little girl. When I was about nine or ten, I stopped going to Kelvenne with my family in the summer. They still all went, but I said I did not want to. Instead I stayed with my grandparents in town. They were both working so I had the place to myself. I loved it. My grandmother gave me some money to buy sweets or go to the swimming pool and I could do just whatever I wanted, which suited me perfectly. And then my grandparents made a great fuss of me. I was like a princess. It's a wonder I wasn't completely spoiled and grew up as an impossibly selfish egoist. Or maybe I did!'

'Not at all,' I exclaimed. 'You're a very kind and generous woman.'

'Well, thank you, Len. What a nice compliment. Even if I did go fishing for it a bit.' She gave me a mischievous grin. 'Yes,' she went on, 'that was another of the differences between me and Esko. As a child and a teenager, he was never very independent. From quite a young age, I was always keen to go to see other places and meet other people. Esko was somehow hyperactive and passive at the same time. I had more opportunities to get out and about, but I think it was also partly that I made them for myself. I asked my uncle Juhani and aunt Raili to take me with them in their boat. Or I went to stay with my other aunts and uncles, and with Ulla. I never wanted to stay at home or in any place that was already familiar.

'And then, when I was seventeen, I went inter-railing across Europe to Paris with one of my girlfriends. My father had fixed me up with a summer job at a local factory where he knew one of the managers, which was really not the way I wanted to spend the summer. I was very angry with him, actually, because he made the arrangement and told his manager friend that I would take the job, without ever asking me if I wanted it. That was very much like him. He would dominate without realizing that he was doing it. It was his default mode. He'd get an idea and assume it must be all fine for everyone else. Of course, he also believed that he was helping me. I'd be able to earn some money. A lot of kids would have been very pleased. But I knew he would not let me go inter-railing. So I set off one morning as if for work, met my friend at the train station, got a train to Helsinki and a boat to Stockholm and telephoned home from there. God, he was angry. But it was too late for him to do anything. Esko would never have done that. Esko would first have got blazing drunk and then marched into the house and announced he was

92

off to Paris and then he would have fallen over and cut his leg open on something. Not that Esko would have wanted to go to Paris in the first place, but you get the picture of the difference between us.'

'Well, what happened when you got back from your trip?'

'I lost my job.'

'Yes, right…'

Päivi laughed. 'The job was long gone, of course. Oh, we had some very uncomfortable days, then a couple of rather bad tempered and silent weeks, then some weeks of avoiding the subject, and little by little we got back to normal. I was in my last year at high school and doing quite well, and the final exams were on the horizon with the prospect of me going to university.

'Do you know, I'd never really thought about this before, but my going off like that was some kind of turning point in my relationship with my father. He didn't treat me like a child after that. It was like he acknowledged me as an independent adult. It was maybe a bit hard for him to accept at first, and he would never have granted the recognition if I had tried to negotiate it. But when I just went ahead and took it I think he saw more clearly who I was. Maybe he even saw how much like him I was and realized it was better not to fight against it. I guess he went through quite a learning process in those years, what with Esko and me. But he was dead chuffed when I got a place at university. Is that the right expression, *chuffed*?'

'Ah, I think it's used in Britain, but you don't hear it in America. It sounds like something John Lennon might have said, *I was dead chuffed*.'

'Poor John. I mean the *dead* bit, not the *chuffed*. Oh, that was wicked. I shouldn't have said that. It really was horribly tragic, the way he died. So senseless.'

93

Chapter Ten

A few hours later, early in the evening on the day of our arrival at the cottage, we went to set fishing nets. Both Aino and Päivi seemed to be quite expert at handling the nets. They'd obviously done it many times. We used the outboard motor to get to the place that Aino reckoned should provide us with a catch and I was then put in charge of the oars as the nets were carefully paid out and arranged properly in the water. We were after vendace, Aino said, and we would come back in the middle of the following morning to check the nets.

'If we have a good catch, we smoke them,' she added.

Sure enough, when we lifted the nets out the next day there were about forty or fifty small silver fish. Vendace, just as Aino had predicted. She clearly knew this water well. We hauled the nets into the boat and headed back to the shore where the nets were hung from a frame and we extracted the fish and collected them in a large bucket. Then Aino gathered some alder branches. She stripped off their bark with a sheath knife and hacked shavings from them with an axe that she'd sharpened on a circular grinding stone till the edge of the blade glistened.

I offered to help with some of the work but the two women exchanged a glance, Aino said something in Finnish and Päivi immediately suggested that she and I go to collect juniper twigs, the other important ingredient in the smoke box. I reckoned they didn't want me slicing my finger off. When we got back with the juniper, the fire was already lit and blazing and the alder shavings were spread over the bottom of the metal box. Aino added the juniper and a lump of sugar – 'To give the fish a brown colour,' Päivi informed me – and then laid the fish out on the wire mesh inside the smoke box. When the flames had burned down and the embers were glowing, she placed the box over it and we sat down to wait. The smell of the scented wood smoke circled round us. After some twenty minutes Aino removed the box and opened it. The taste of those vendace, hot from the smoking box, is with me still, emblematic of those summer days and lakeside scenery. It was one of the tastiest meals I've ever eaten.

When we had returned from setting the nets that first evening, we lit a fire in the stove of what was known as the beach sauna. I was entrusted with the task of keeping it fed with wood until the sauna was hot enough, and then Aino and Päivi took their turn first while I sat on the cottage veranda looking at the still lake scenery, out towards where the nets were. The sun was not then low enough to color the sky, but the clouds had already begun to break up and there were patches of blue. The women disappeared inside the sauna building down near the lake shore and I fell into a peaceful trance.

After perhaps fifteen minutes two figures emerged from the sauna, stepped down to the lake and began to wade out into the water. They were both completely naked. There was about thirty or forty yards between us. Their figures were significantly diminished by the distance, but even so, nothing was left to the imagination, as the saying is. I sat and stared for a second or two in utter amazement but that feeling was rapidly replaced by a mixture of guilt and embarrassment. I felt as if I'd been caught in a reprehensible act. My next reaction was to look away, and then to move myself to a position where we would be out of sight of each other. I felt as if I *ought* to move away. Not to do so would be like peeping. I started to rise from my seat. By this time the women were already in the water. Only their heads were visible. Päivi waved from the lake. I waved back and kept my seat. For the time being, at least, I told myself, I was safe.

'Safe,' I muttered to myself. 'What on earth do I mean by that?' The women knew that I was sitting on the veranda. They must have known that I'd be looking towards the lake. They were simply quite unselfconscious about their nakedness. In a few minutes, maybe even seconds, they would leave the water and return to the sauna. 'If I stay and watch, am I peeping, or just being natural and unconcerned, as they are?' I wondered as I tried to decide how best to act.

'The bare-assed cheek of it,' I murmured to myself, just audibly, and chuckled. That chuckle was a laugh at myself and it restored my sense of proportion. What a fuss I'd been making.

Then I began to imagine how such a scene as I'd just witnessed would be received in America. The reaction of the American women in my circle of acquaintance, if they had been seen in such a state of undress, would have been one of exaggerated distress. Their condemnation of women acting as Aino and Päivi had just done would have been extreme. Yet there had been nothing coquettish in their behavior. They hadn't been flaunting themselves in front of me in any way. Just using those words in my thoughts brought home how inappropriate they were. I thought of Helen. She would have been quite hysterical if a man had seen her naked. Her language about such behavior as I had just encountered would have been as uncomplimentary as it could be. And she would have been quite scathing about my conclusion that Päivi and Aino were simply being unselfconscious.

'You men don't see what's in front of your noses,' would have been Helen's reply. It's one of her favorite expressions.

With some surprise, I suddenly realized how little I had thought of Helen during the last few days. It was true that I didn't miss her. I was glad that she wasn't here. To do myself justice, that was due partly to my awareness that she wouldn't have been enjoying the experiences that had meant so much to me, but it was also because I would not have wished for her company now myself.

At this point, my meditations were interrupted. Aino and Päivi were leaving the water. As their bodies appeared above the surface they wrapped their arms around themselves to partly hide themselves and, reaching the land, quickly half-ran into the sauna.

When the women had finished and returned to the cottage, it was my turn to use the sauna. I collected my towel, a change of clothes and swimsuit. I sat in the hot room, sweating and turning over my choices - swim naked, swim with my swimsuit, don't swim at all. I opted for a very short sauna. I didn't bother to go into the lake. There was a barrel of cool water in the corner that I could mix with a little of the boiling water from the stove tank and wash in. I didn't need the lake. Better to get back quickly for the supper that was being prepared, I told myself.

After we'd eaten and cleared up, we sat on the veranda. By this time the clouds had almost entirely cleared, with only a few scattered wisps remaining. We sat there watching the sun stain those bits of cloud orange and pink while the sky over the pine trees was reflected in the still lake. The scene was so tranquil that talking felt like a disturbance.

But, although tranquil, it was full of activity. In silence we observed all that was going on. All over the surface of the water rings were constantly appearing, expanding, disappearing. Occasionally there would be a soft splash and a slightly wider disturbance. Small flies and mosquitoes circled round us, some lost interest, others didn't. From time to time, one of us flicked a hand casually past an ear. Very gradually the light drained away under the trees and the surface of the water became faintly luminous.

Now and then a faint, secretive rustle came from the forest. After one louder scuffling in the undergrowth, Aino murmured, 'Supikoira.'

'Racoon dog,' Päivi added.

A few bats could be seen gliding out from the trees that bordered the lake, twisting and weaving as they caught flies. At one point a larger shape glided between the birch trunks. I thought at first that it was heading straight for us but that was the dimness deceiving my eye, it was passing us diagonally. I thought it must be a larger species of bat; by its wingspan, much larger. Suddenly, it dropped to the ground, a shrill scream pierced the air, then the owl rose up, a couple of flaps of its wings as it glided past, silhouetted against the shining water, a dead mouse visible in its talons. For much of that last hour we sat in silence.

Chapter Eleven

The next day, after our lunch of smoked vendace, we went on the trip to Kelvenne. Aino wanted to stay behind at the cottage, she said. There were two birch trees that had been felled and were lying at one side of the plot. Päivi explained that Aino planned to cut and chop them for firewood. She was going to get started on the job while we went to Kelvenne.

'Aino felled the trees some three or four weeks ago and they've been lying long enough now.'

'But you don't mean that the wood will be dry, surely.'

'Well, pretty nearly. It's a method which is called *kaataa lehdekseen* in Finnish. It means that you fell the tree just at the moment in spring when the leaf buds are beginning to open and then let the tree lie for a couple of weeks or so. During that time the leaves continue to open and grow and that process requires a lot of water which the leaves draw from the trunk of the tree. Usually, of course, the tree would be drawing water from the ground to supply the leaves, but when the tree is felled the water is literally sucked out of the wood, drying it. The spring was very late this year so the leaf buds were late, too, but even so those two birch trees must have been lying there somewhat longer than three or four weeks actually; longer than was really necessary, in fact. Aino's going to saw the trunks into sections while we're on Kelvenne and then chop the logs today or tomorrow and stack them and it will be possible to use them as firewood, or in the sauna, within a week. If the wood was wet, it would take the whole summer and more to get them dry enough to burn well.'

'Amazing. You Finns really know what you're doing, don't you?'

Päivi smiled. 'Well, actually a lot of Finns have never heard of *kaataa lehdekseen*. Those who live in the towns have lost a lot of the knowledge of how to handle nature. A hundred years ago everyone would have known it.'

As Päivi and I headed down towards the shore, Aino was beginning work, wearing a helmet and visor and heavy gloves and wielding a motor saw that whined as the blade cut into the first tree.

The day was fairly still. A very light, steady breeze just ruffled the surface of the lake, breaking up the reflections of the forest along the shoreline. We launched the small dinghy, started the motor and set off towards Kelvenne.

The island was barely fifty yards wide at the point where we made landfall. We pulled the boat up onto the sandy shore and Päivi led the way through the trees, heading southwards. From the top of the ridge, we could see several other boats along the shore, some larger cabin cruisers moored off-shore and dinghies like ours pulled out of the water. Some figures were settled on a small sandy beach round one bay. We walked on.

'I want to show you the lagoons that I told you about,' Päivi said over her shoulder.

'Great. I'm really keen to see them,' I replied.

We walked perhaps half a mile along the ridge, then started to descend towards the right-hand shore. I could see the water, dark between the trees. As we reached the edge the whole of the first lagoon came into full view. It was as Päivi had described. The bank sloped steeply into the water. The rim was sandy but you couldn't call it a beach because it was so narrow and sloping. The sand extended underwater, but the bottom sloped down so steeply that it disappeared from sight only a yard or so from the edge. The water was strongly colored a very dark brown. It was remarkably still and quiet. We stood for a while in silence, just absorbing the atmosphere.

'These lagoons were made at the end of the Ice Age,' Päivi began.

'I learned something about that on my lake cruise,' I said. 'The guide explained how the present landscape in this area was formed by the glaciers moving and carving out the shape of the terrain.'

'Yes, that's right. The sheets of ice could be several kilometers thick and they literally scraped away the surface of the land. They scraped off the tops of a mountain range in this area. And then, when the ice was melting, the meltwater drained down through cracks and fissures in the glaciers and literally bored into the rock, gravel and sand beneath. Over hundreds of years, I think, maybe a thousand even, I don't know exactly. That's what must have happened here. The flow of the meltwater and the sand, gravel and stones that it carried with it bored and scoured these craters in the land which filled up with water as the lake was formed. These lagoons are very deep. I don't know exactly how deep.'

We'd been slowly wandering along the top edge of the slope above the lagoon, but now Päivi began to edge down the steep bank towards the water. I followed behind her, slipping in places where the surface of the ground was loose and sandy.

'Careful,' Päivi warned. 'If you lose your balance here, you will end up in the water.'

'Making a splash.'

There were a few slim birch trees half way down the bank which we could hold on to give ourselves a bit more control on our descent. At last we arrived safely down at the strip of sand. It was fine and soft, so that our feet sank into it.

'Our guide on the cruise told us that Finland is still rising after the weight of the ice has left the land. The ice pressed the surface rock into the bedrock for thousands of years

101

and after that weight was removed the surface rock is sort of rebounding back in very slow motion.'

'That's right,' Päivi replied. 'A large part of the archipelago between Finland and Sweden has risen up out of the sea over the last … 6,000 years, I believe it is. There are several archaeological sites that are known to have been originally on the mainland coast and are now well inland. Much of Ostrobothnia is former sea bed. They even say that someone from those coastal areas who lives to be ninety or a hundred years old can walk in old age where they swam as a child.'

'It gives you a strange feeling, doesn't it, to know that the world that we see around us every day, the features of the landscape that we take for granted are the product of processes that take tens of thousands of years to complete. And that the changes are still going on. They will never stop, I suppose. Nature never says, *Right, now that's finished and ready.*'

'It makes our lives and concerns appear very small and unimportant, doesn't it?'

'Yes, in one way, when you think on that vast scale. But still the scale of human life is the one that we really feel in our backbone. It's important, too.'

'Yes, Len, you're right about that.'

We wandered a little way along the shore, almost slipping into the water as the sand moved under our weight, then climbed back up to the top of the slope and sat a while on the slope above the lagoon without speaking.

'Come on,' Päivi said, 'I'll show you the beach where we used to make our camp.'

We set off, past the second lagoon, and came to an area where the gradient was less steep towards the water. The higher part of the ridge was steeper and more thickly wooded, but as the land came down towards the lake it was more open and there was a large flat area behind a relatively wide stretch of beach. We walked all along it and Päivi pointed out the places where they'd built their tents and played and done all the things that she'd told me about. She even thought that she'd found the rock, at one end of the beach, which they had heated by making a fire in a pit underneath it and then used as a sauna.

'I'm sure this must be it,' she said.

We examined it, trying to find some indication that there had been a fire under it but there were no marks left. Then we went back along the beach to a convenient spot where we took off our shoes, rolled up the cuffs of our pants and paddled in the shallow water. Decidedly chilly at first, it was, but pleasant once you'd gotten used to it. Our feet sank into the fine, soft sand under the water. I wriggled my toes in it. The feeling was quite sensuous.

We stayed a couple of hours on Kelvenne and then returned to the dinghy and motored back to Aino's cottage in time for afternoon coffee and a snack. Being so much in the fresh air made me feel always ready to eat. Aino had also been busy. Both of the birch trees had been sawn into sections ready to be chopped into logs, a job that I was allowed to help with later. The ground was covered with sawdust where she'd been working, and already there was a constantly running line of large forest ants with fat, dark red bodies, the color of congealed blood, carrying the grains away to their nest somewhere under the trees.

As I watched, I noticed that a couple of ants were carrying a small, yellowish caterpillar between them. It was twisting slightly in their grip. They were taking it to their food store, or whatever ants have in their nest. I felt sorry for it and thought of saving it from a horrible fate, but then I decided I shouldn't interfere with nature's processes. I straightened up and began to walk away, but after just a few steps I went back and rescued the caterpillar. I reckoned that I was also part of nature's process and the ants would surely survive okay without that one caterpillar.

'Do you like chanterelles, Len?' Aino asked as we ate hard boiled eggs and anchovies on rye bread.

'I love them,' I replied.

'Päivi can show where to pick them up. If you bring enough, I can make a soup.'

So after our light meal, Päivi and I set off with a small plastic bucket to collect chanterelles.

'There are several good spots to find them,' Päivi explained as we headed away from the cottage, through the forest. We followed a small path for some way, then left it and walked between the trees to where the land began to rise gently. 'This is one place where we could find some,' she said. 'They are often half concealed under other plants and undergrowth. You have to look very carefully.'

There were plenty of mushrooms around, but we were interested only in chanterelles. We went side-by-side, a few feet apart and scanned the ground carefully. It was a real thrill to find them, nestling half-hidden amongst the grass or moss. They're a brilliant, butter-yellow and the shape is so elegant, like a fluted trumpet. I felt a thrill every time I found one, like finding a nugget of gold, a gift from the forest gods.

'They tend to grow in colonies,' Päivi said, 'so when you find one you will probably find others.'

'There's something quite baroque about them,' I commented, when we'd just finished clearing one fairly large colony. I held one on my palm. It was almost weightless. 'If Bach had been a mushroom, he would have been a chanterelle,' I added.

Päivi giggled with delight. 'That's a lovely saying, Len. *If Bach had been a mushroom.* I must remember that.'

Later, when our bucket was full enough and we were already on our homeward route, Päivi stooped down beside a large patch of thick and luxuriant moss.

'I love moss,' she said simply. 'It symbolizes the slow and eternal to me. The moss that grows around Aino's plot never seems to change. It doesn't spread and it doesn't recede. It's just always the same, year after year. It's the antithesis of change, and of decision-making. All those hectic elements that we seem to have gotten into our lives.'

She reached out and gently stroked it with the back of one hand and then brushed it with her fingertips. I can't explain why, but my imagination spontaneously turned the moss that Päivi was stroking into pubic hair. I watched her fingers move gently across the moss and I couldn't help imagining my own fingers moving through her pubic hair in the same way. Just at that moment, this strange image didn't bother me at all, though when I considered it later it troubled me a good deal.

'It's so delicate,' she went on, 'yet it survives the winters and half a meter of snow. So delicate, yet so tenacious.'

'Like you,' I murmured.

'Me? I'm not delicate.'

'To me, you are.'

We looked at each other in silence for a moment. A charged moment. Then we both blushed like a couple of teenagers. Then we laughed to dispel the tension.

'….but I *am* tenacious,' she added, and the moment had passed.

When we got back to the cottage we showed Aino what the forest had provided.

'It is enough,' she said. 'I make chanterelle soup. We eat it after sauna.'

Aino was a woman of few words, but all of them to the point. She spoke with a noticeably monotone and rather clipped delivery. It was the same if she was speaking

Finnish or English. Her English was limited but she was always ready with a phrase, an explanation, a comment in English to help to keep me in the picture. Often, when the conversation was going on in Finnish and I was completely out of it, and Päivi hadn't translated anything for a while, Aino would say two short sentences in English that summarized the issue under discussion. You know that writing exercise that schoolkids do, when they're given a passage of 600 words, say, and they have to reproduce all the essential information in just 300 words? Précis, it's called. Well, Aino could do it verbally, spontaneously reducing five minutes of debate to its essence in two sentences.

She had an uncanny way of knowing what I was thinking, too. Several times it happened, when Päivi was translating for me, and the discussion moved through various stages until one detail or aspect of the issue set me wondering or feeling doubtful, Aino would drop a comment or fact, in English, into the conversation that exactly answered to whatever it was that had been disturbing me. A good example occurred on the day of the chanterelle gathering. Aino had mentioned having the soup after the sauna and the suggestion was then made by Päivi that we should all go to the sauna together.

'It would be more sociable,' she explained. 'You wouldn't have to wait on your own, Len, while we had our sauna, and then have to take yours alone.'

I liked the sociability side of it, but the suggestion sent my pulse rate up in an unpleasant manner. I wasn't sure if I could deal with the nudity; theirs and mine. It had been all very well to joke myself out of embarrassment the evening before, at a distance, with all *my* clothes on. Stripping off, all together, in a confined space was a different matter. But I didn't want to make a fuss about something that they seemed to take so matter-of-factly. And I didn't want to refuse and look priggish. I was starting to feel in a bit of a corner.

'We wear swimsuits and make it not too hot,' Aino observed quietly.

All my fears were dispelled, although I've never been able to work out whether she meant 'not too hot' to refer simply to the temperature.

Yes, I was glad that Aino, with her seeming ability to guess my thoughts, hadn't witnessed that little scene with Päivi stroking the moss and me looking on. Before the end of my time in Finland I came to feel a deep respect for Aino, admiration even.

'You're going to love Aino's chanterelle soup,' Päivi said after our communal sauna. 'It's special.'

'How's it made?' I asked.

'The secret is to add whipped egg whites to the soup just before serving it. Not many people know the recipe, or they can't do it right. It's important that you don't let it boil after adding the egg whites. They give the soup a texture like foam. It's delicious.'

This was no exaggeration. I can't describe the experience of eating that soup. The flavor was wonderfully delicate, the chanterelles were chopped so finely that there was almost nothing to chew, but still there were solids in the texture. I could say that it was like mushroom-flavored liquid meringue, that's as close as words can come.

It was usually quite late when we separated for the night, Aino and Päivi sharing one of the bedrooms, me going to the other. My room was dim, but not dark. It was scarcely dusk at midnight. Under the trees it was fairly dark, but the lake still reflected the last light from the sky. That night I lay in bed and remembered the scene with Päivi in the woods that afternoon. I had told her that she was delicate to me. Now that I was on my own to contemplate this, I began to feel more than a little foolish. What on earth had I been saying? And fantasizing about stroking her pubic hair. Jesus Christ! I must be losing my senses completely.

I tried to calm myself down and think rationally about this. It didn't require an awful lot of thought, to be honest. I was becoming attached, romantically attached, to Päivi. That was the simple truth. In my thoughts I used the term 'romantically attached' rather than 'falling in love', so as to make it *not too hot*, as Aino might have said. This admission disturbed me a good deal. She was my second cousin and that felt too close for comfort. Afterwards came the thought that I was a married man with a family. And finally, the cold fact that I was in this country for three weeks and my whole life was on the other side of the planet.

That night I slept very badly. If I'm frank, that was mainly because I was so conscious of Päivi on the other side of the wall.

Chapter Twelve

The next morning I came out onto the veranda after breakfast and, seeing Päivi standing at one end of it, I walked towards her, starting to make some comment or other but she half-turned her head with her finger to her lips to show that I should come softly. I tip-toed the last part of the way.

'What is it?' I whispered.

'A hare,' she replied, indicating the direction.

There it was, crouched in the grass and weeds at the edge of the open area, nibbling at the vegetation. Its lips and teeth worked quickly and sensitively, its nostrils twitching all the while. When it bit off a longer stalk that was left dangling, it lifted its head slightly, chewing and working the length of stalk into its mouth with a trance-like gaze in its great, round eyes that were hypnotic, so that we were also in a trance: entranced by the hare. Then it bent down again and continued eating. It stretched its head as far forward as it could to find fresh growth and only when it couldn't reach any further did it extend its long back legs, raise its hind quarters and half hop, half hobble forward a pace with an awkward, ungainly gait. When it moved like that, its rear legs looked too long, and its back sloped down to its shoulders and the shorter front legs. Then it sank its plump hind quarters back to the ground, with a fluid motion, sitting like a liquid drop that has come to rest. Several times it moved forward in this way, sniffing the air and swiveling its ears from time to time. We watched it in silence until it suddenly seemed to become aware of us, or something else, perhaps. It straightened all four legs instantly and stood taut for a moment, listening. Then it was off, bounding between the trees and out of sight.

'Lovely,' I murmured.

'Isn't it?' Päivi replied. 'I love to watch them, the way they move and eat and just sit so still.'

'In many cultures they're regarded as having some kind of mystical quality.'

'So I've heard.'

'The Celts believed they had. When the Celtic Queen Boadicea was about to go into battle against the Roman army one time, a hare ran through the Celtic camp. Boadicea wouldn't let her soldiers kill the animal to eat. She said it was a good omen.'

'What happened?'

'They lost the battle, actually.'

'I like them just for themselves. It's very calming to watch a hare. In fact, I think it's very calming to watch any wild animal in its own habitat.'

'I guess you're right. It's not something I've ever done much back home.'

'But there's plenty of forest and wilderness around where you live, surely.'

'Yes, but I've never spent a lot of time in it. And you'd have to go quite some way out of St Paul to find forest as dense and extensive as this.'

'You've gotten too used to the big city life, Len.'

Later in the day Taru, Liisa and Heikki, Liisa's husband, visited the cottage. They arrived around noon and as soon as the car had stopped, Taru was out, leaving the car door wide open, and made her way straight to the cottage door where Aino, Päivi and I were already waiting. I was introduced to her and we shook hands.

'Hauska tutustua,' I articulated as best I could, though it sounded very slurred to my own ear and probably much more so to a Finnish one.

'Oh, you speak Finnish,' Taru said.

110

'Well, not really,' I admitted. 'Päivi has just taught me how to greet people and I've been practicing how to pronounce it right for the last two days.'

'But that's wonderful. You said it very well. Come and listen to Len speak Finnish,' she called to Liisa and Heikki, who were just now coming up to the front door.

Beginning to feel a little self-conscious, I shook hands with them and repeated my Finnish greeting. They responded with a softly-spoken return of the greeting, which would have been the end of the little ceremony, but Taru started up again.

'Doesn't he say it well?' she demanded.

'It was very nicely spoken, Len,' Liisa said.

'Do you have a program for studying Finnish?' Taru asked me.

'Oh heavens, no,' I replied. 'I don't have any such grand plans. A word or two to try to be polite when meeting people is the full extent of my ambition.'

'But you must have a program and a carefully planned timetable. I can work out a study plan and send it to you. And you must stick to it. That is the only way to make progress in learning anything.'

I'm sure she meant well, but she didn't seem to have taken in the fact that I'd just told her I didn't plan to study Finnish beyond a few phrases. Liisa and Heikki waited, without adding anything further, looking from Taru to me and back. The silence extended. I felt that the situation was becoming increasingly awkward until Aino urged us all to come inside the cottage.

'I left the family at home,' Taru began, once we were inside. 'The children had their own affairs, of course. Off with their friends somewhere. And Jaakko – that's my husband, Len – has been saying for weeks that he's going to....to...erm... remontoida?' she said, glancing towards Päivi.

111

'Renovate,' Päivi said.

'….renovate the spare bedroom. Right, I said to him, now you can start it, while I go to meet my American cousin. And so he's doing it now.'

Aino had prepared coffee with sandwiches and cake which we ate on the back veranda. At first, the conversation consisted mainly of them asking me questions about my life. I told them where I lived, what family I had, what job I did. All the usual details. They wanted to hear what memories I had of my grandparents and particularly about my grandfather, who was the brother of Taru's grandfather and Liisa's father. So we chatted on. Taru's English was good: very fluent and reasonably accurate. Liisa and Heikki seemed a little less confident, but they understood everything and asked questions sometimes and made some comments. And so we got along very nicely.

After the refreshments, we stretched our legs a bit. We ambled down to the shore, looked across the lake and threw some stones into the water. At one point I found myself standing with Taru a little apart from the others.

'So what do you do for a living, Taru?' I asked.

'I teach in a kindergarten.'

Immediately she said it, I could just imagine Taru in that role, she had the right personality for it. And I'm sure she's very good at it, too.

'You and Päivi are in the same sort of profession, then,' I said.

'Yes, in a way. But Päivi, of course, has a university training and we kindergarten teachers are just considered as vocational staff. I wanted to go to university, too, but there was no place for me.'

I sensed that there was a bit of an edge to this last comment and I reckoned it was time to change the subject.

'Päivi and I went to Kelvenne yesterday,' I said, remembering that Taru had also been there during those summer holidays that Päivi had told me about. 'I think that's a place you know well, too, from your childhood, right?'

'Oh, Kelvenne, yes. We spent our summers there as children, with Liisa and her sister and parents, too.'

'Päivi's told me all about it. It sounds idyllic. Did you and Päivi spend a lot of time together as children?'

'Oh yes. There were a lot of us cousins and we were often together. Me and my brothers, and Päivi and Esko were often together because our fathers were brothers.'

'Päivi has told me something about her skiing when she was a youngster. Did you also ski a lot, Taru?'

'Oh, yes. I loved skiing. I still do. I used to go to all the races, like Päivi, and I often won.'

'You seem to have a talent for skiing in your family. You must both have been pretty good.'

'We were. There's one year between us, so we weren't always in the same races, but sometimes we were.'

'Who won then?' I asked, with a smile.

'Sometimes me, sometimes Päivi.'

There was a rather curt tone to Taru's last reply which warned me off pursuing this topic, but it was too late.

'We were both good skiers, but Päivi was always the favorite. Of course, her daddy was one of the club officials and on the board of the local skiing association, so what can you expect?'

I started casting about for a new topic, but I couldn't think of anything quickly.

'She always had the best training and her skis were waxed better than anybody else's. I could have been just as good as her, but I had no one to direct my training and tell me the right tactics for each course. But anyway, that's all in the past, now. And Päivi never got to be the national champion, like her daddy wanted.'

113

I was starting to get a bit desperate, isolated in this conversation, when luckily the rest of the party joined us and Taru proposed that we should go into the forest to collect some berries.

'I have got two buckets with me that I want to fill,' she added.

'Make sure you have rain clothes, it is going to rain this afternoon,' Aino added.

'No, it won't rain,' Taru replied. 'Come on everyone. Let's go into the forest.'

We had to get ourselves kitted out first. It wasn't cold, but there was a bit of a breeze that gave a chill to the air and it seemed wise to heed Aino's warning of rain. Liisa and Heikki had waterproof jackets in their car. Aino, Päivi and I found outer garments in the cottage. I had to borrow an old anorak as I didn't have anything suitable with me. Taru stood at the front of the cottage with a bright red bucket in each hand.

'Come along in there,' she called.

We all set off into the forest, at first following about the same route as we had done on the chanterelle picking trip, but then branching off in a different direction. Before long I was quite lost, but we soon came to a place where the forest floor was covered with blueberry bushes. I had a small beaker to collect the berries in, which I tipped into one of Taru's buckets when I'd filled it. I didn't need the berries for myself, of course, and Aino said she already had plenty and could always collect more if she wanted later in the summer. She and Päivi also tipped the berries they collected into Taru's buckets. They grow very low and picking them requires bending down close to the ground. It's rather back-breaking work and after a short while my work-rate slowed considerably. I spent more time chatting and looking around me, observing the different types of plant. There were a great many varieties of mushroom.

114

Some looked very appetizing. I asked about the edibility of several and some we were able to pick as good for eating. And then there were the overgrown mushrooms that had started to decay; huge, slimy monsters with an unpleasant odor like rotten meat.

At one point Päivi and I had moved a little apart from the others.

'How have you been getting on with Taru?' Päivi asked.

I glanced at her. She had a decidedly mischievous grin on her lips.

'Erm, fine,' I said, trying to be non-committal.

'She doesn't mean any harm, but she sometimes talks a lot and says things without really thinking. And she can seem a bit domineering and bossy. I think that might be partly because she has worked in a kindergarten, with very small children, for so many years. You have to be a bit like that with small kids. She's not so good at imagining situations from other people's points of view and she's very direct. What I'm saying is, that she doesn't always realize the effect of her comments or actions.'

'Yes, I think I know what you mean. Like when she made a bit too much of my trying to speak Finnish when they arrived.'

'Exactly. I hope you weren't annoyed.'

'Good lord, no. It was nothing.'

'Oh good. We're so used to her that we take her as she is, but I know that she can be too much for some people.'

'Put your mind at rest, Päivi.'

'She sometimes gets a bit competitive with me, actually,' Päivi went on. 'It's as if she feels that she has to prove herself. I can't think why she takes me as the standard to measure herself against. Oh well.'

I didn't mention Taru's comments about the skiing competitions but I guessed that Päivi would have heard similar comments many times before.

'We've gotten a bit left behind,' Päivi added, glancing towards the rest of the group as they picked their way between the trees.

'You said "gotten".'

'Hmm?'

'You just said, "we've gotten". You've started to use American expressions. I noticed it once or twice before. You must've picked them up from me.'

'Really? Well, I suppose it's not so surprising. Perhaps I'll develop an American accent, too, before you leave.'

'It's funny, because earlier I'd been thinking that you spoke just the way the English do and now you're starting to sound American.'

'Yeah, I know I speak a very English kind of English. I guess it's because I spent a lot of time in England when I was young. I was about nine months in an English family as an au pair during my gap year. And then when I was studying English at university I spent several summers working in England and went to Sussex University as an exchange student. I even had an English boyfriend for a few years, which is one of the reasons I was so keen to go and stay there. But come on. We should catch up with the others.'

We'd filled our beakers some time ago and now went to empty them into Taru's bucket. With three others, in addition to Taru herself, contributing their haul, the buckets were filling fairly rapidly, even though my contribution was rather slight. We moved forward slowly all the time, over a rise and down a slope. Water became visible between the trees. We moved along roughly parallel to it for some way and then came to a place where the forest was less dense and the lake more clearly seen between the trees. Standing upright after a short bout of picking, I stretched, deposited my meager load in the bucket and strolled down to the lakeside to look at the

116

view. As I came out into the open space on the shore and a wider expanse of sky came into view, I got a bit of a shock to see that it was more than half covered with a solid bank of dark, bluish-grey cloud that seemed to promise thunder. I hurried back to the others to tell them what I'd just seen.

'Oh, I saw that cloud ages ago,' Taru replied, 'but I didn't say anything because I wanted to get these buckets filled.'

'They're full now,' Aino said. 'We go this way back to the cottage.' And she set off immediately.

We'd gone only a hundred yards or so when the first heavy drop of rain landed with a splat on my shoulder. Within a couple of minutes we were in the middle of a downpour. There was nowhere to shelter. The trees offered very little. We put our hoods over our heads and kept walking. The thunder crashed around us. It grew quite dim under the trees and the rain streamed down my face and the anorak and soaked my pants. Luckily, I had on a pair of rubber boots that Aino had found for me so my feet were dry.

When we got back to the cottage we had to get out of our wet clothes. Our top jackets were quickly removed and hung up to dry and warm jumpers handed round. In addition to the summer cottage being a destination for superannuated furniture, it was also the place where all old clothes that had been rejected for town use were taken. There were plenty of old jackets, jumpers, spare rubber boots and so on. We who were staying in the cottage had our own dry things to put on, of course. Taru had brought a spare pair of jeans with her and changed into them. Liisa borrowed some old corduroy pants from Aino. Heikki reckoned that his pants were semi-waterproof. He was wearing a sort of outdoor suit made of a canvas type of material. He said it was designed for this kind of country use and that the material was shower-proof, but not really

117

adequate in such heavy rain. However, he said that he wasn't too wet and would dry off pretty quickly.

'Now we need some hot coffee and cognac,' Aino said when we were all dry and settled. 'Except poor Heikki, because he is driving.'

Heikki pulled a rueful expression and we all laughed and commiserated with him.

By the time the coffee was made and poured the storm had passed over. We went out onto the back veranda. Now and again the rumble of thunder would reach us, sounding faintly in the distance as the storm moved up the lake. Across the water, one section of the far shore was vividly illuminated, like a scene in a painting. Where the sun shone through a break in the clouds, the brightly lit strip of land stood out against the hard, metal-dark sky, the opposite of a silhouette, I guess you could say.

Chapter Thirteen

The next day Päivi and I planned to leave the cottage and return to Hämeenlinna.

'Why don't we go by way of Kuhmalahti,' Päivi suggested, 'and try to find some information about that Joosepi Virtanen who moved there in 1944? After all, we're already half way to Kuhmalahti here. It would make sense to go now, rather than making a special trip from Hämeenlinna.'

I was in full agreement with the idea so after a leisurely breakfast and packing our things we said goodbye to Aino, who had her own car with her, and set off for Kuhmalahti.

We spent a couple of hours with the parish records, and found Joosepi and his wife, Jaana, and their five children, all of whom were added to the Virtanen side of my family tree.

Around one o'clock we were getting kind of hungry. Kuhmalahti didn't boast much in the way of restaurants, but we found a small place, more like a café, that offered hot snacks.

'There was quite a baby boom in Finland in the years after the war,' Päivi said when we were seated with our lunch. She was referring to the several births in Joosepi's and Jaana's family in those years. 'That's the right term, isn't it? That generation are called the baby boomers, aren't they?'

'Yes, that's right,' I confirmed.

'And Joosepi's uncle, Paavo, died in 1918, did you notice?'

'Yes. The same year that my grandfather's brother, Arto, died. Päivi, the day that you met me at Hämeenlinna railroad station and drove me to the hotel, you mentioned something about the civil war that was fought in Finland in

119

that year. Do you know if there's a connection between those two deaths and that fighting?'

'Well, I don't know anything about Joosepi Virtanen and his family. I've only recently discovered his existence…'

'Yes, of course.'

'…but I do know the details of Arto's death. It's rather disturbing, I'm afraid,' she added, glancing at me.

'I'd like to know.'

'Yes, I thought you would.' She paused for a moment, then went on. 'Your grandfather's twin brother was executed.'

'Executed! My God! Why? What did he do?'

'It happened a lot during the civil war. On both sides. The story's been handed down in the family, always in hushed voices, and it wasn't spoken of outside the family. It's a long way in the past now, of course, but I remember as a child hearing about it and it was still a very difficult topic then. One of his brothers and two of his sisters were still alive at that time, of course.

'Well, Arto fought on the red side in the civil war. Before the fighting began he was very active in the socialist organization. There were various protests and actions against the big farmers and landowners. Arto was well known as quite a radical, apparently. When the situation deteriorated to the level of civil war, each side regarded the most active or vocal representatives of the other side as criminals. When prisoners were taken there were investigations to establish what 'crimes' they had been involved in. Arto was captured and he was sufficiently well known for charges to be brought against him. He was actually charged with murdering a big landowner out near Hämeenkyrö. Whether he really did it, no one knows. There were plenty of cases at that time of false evidence being sworn to. That's a fact. Several such cases have been

120

proved since. However, so-called witnesses swore that Arto was the man and he was executed by firing squad.'

'That's horrible,' I murmured.

'It is. Obviously, it was a hugely difficult event for the family to come to terms with. Firstly, of course, there was the loss of a son and brother. Secondly, there was the stigma attached to the crime and execution. And thirdly, for his parents, there was the additional difficulty of his having been a red. I don't mean that they supported the white side. I don't think they did, as far as I've understood the facts as they've been handed down. But they were very religious and conservative and I think they felt that socialism, communism, if you want to go that far, was an upsetting of the ordained order of the world. God's order. I think you could say that they believed the reds were wrong, without believing that the whites were right. That's the best way that I can put it. But they believed that the war and killing was wrong on both sides. I've understood that they were deeply grieved for the death of their son, obviously, and horrified that he might have been guilty of the crime he was executed for.'

'I wonder if he was, or if he was just a scapegoat?'

'That's the question. By the time I was old enough to understand what these issues meant, Juhani was the only one of that generation still alive. Mari died when I was only eighteen and I never spoke to her about these matters seriously, as an adult, though she may have been the source of some of those half-remembered, whispered stories from my childhood. She probably was because my own grandfather on my father's side died when my father was still a child. He was one of Arto's brothers, of course. And my father didn't learn anything about the affair from his own parents because he was so young when they died. I talked about it once or twice with my father, but it was all quite remote to him. The only real first-hand information that I've gotten came from my uncle Juhani, but he was only ten years old when Arto died and didn't have very clear memories of him. He did remember some arguments between Arto and their father. He used to say that Arto was hot-tempered and quite a firebrand, but that doesn't make him a murderer. Juhani remembered more of the atmosphere and feelings in the family home immediately after Arto's death. Not surprisingly, it made a deep impression on him. Well, we'll never know now what the truth is.'

'My father's name is Arto.'

'Yes, I know.'

'That's not a coincidence, I guess.'

'I believe your grandfather was very close to his twin brother.'

'Do you know if that's the reason, or partly the reason, why they emigrated? I mean that they wanted to leave those dreadful memories behind?'

'I don't remember that I've ever heard that stated in so many words, but I do remember Juhani saying that in the aftermath of Arto's death, there was some concern that your grandfather might be on the wanted list. He wasn't so active in the socialist movement, but because he was Arto's twin brother and the closeness between the two of them led to their being often linked together, there was the fear that it might just be assumed that he shared his views, or whatever it is that might have been thought to constitute a reason for taking him as well. It was all so mad and horrible at that time. I believe that your grandfather was in hiding at some time immediately after the end of the civil war, when the white side had won.'

'I can imagine it being like that,' I replied. 'And I can just begin to imagine what the fear must have been like. Maybe. I've sure heard plenty of civil war stories back home in America. Experiences like those would be enough to lead

122

anyone to emigrate. My dear old grandparents. How much I never knew about your lives.'

We were silent for a while. My thoughts were in some turmoil. They raced from my own memories of my grandparents, to imagining them leaving Finland with these events fresh in their memories, to imagining Arto standing in front of the firing squad, saying goodbye to life at the age of twenty-three. These thoughts spun round and round in my mind, one continually replacing another and coming back to where I had started.

'It's difficult now to imagine those things happening in Finland,' I said. 'It's such a peaceful, well regulated country. All the time I've been here I keep thinking how sane Finland seems in comparison with America. Or some aspects of it, at least.'

'I hope you're right, Len. But it hasn't always been like this. And for many years after the civil war - and I mean decades - Finnish society was divided along those old political lines. Although technically outlawed, a growing communist element was active all through the 1920s, mainly under the mask of the labor movement, until, in 1930, there was an anti-communist reaction that almost led to another civil war. There were cases of known communist supporters being kidnapped, driven over the Russian border, and left there. Others went of their own accord. A large group of extreme right-wing, armed men actually gathered just north of Helsinki in 1932, seemingly with the intention of carrying out a coup d'état. In the end they dispersed without fighting.'

'Really? I'd never heard about that.'

'Yes. In fact, I can tell you a story to show how divided the country was. As late as the 50s and early 60s, in the village where I grew up, there were two grocery stores: one was a cooperative, which gave it a socialist character, and the other was privately owned by a distant relative of one

123

of the local big landowners. That one had right-wing associations. Each family in the village used only one of those stores, depending on their political sympathies. They would never have gone into the other store. I can remember the shops well, and I knew that I could only use one of them to buy sweets, or if I went on an errand to do some shopping. I didn't understand the reason, but I was in no doubt about the fact. And right into the eighties, there were two national sports associations in Finland: the Workers' Sports Union, which was left-wing, obviously, and the Finnish National Sports Association, which was right-wing. Every sports club in the country was affiliated to one or the other. By the nineteen-eighties, people, especially the younger generation, were paying less and less attention to the political implications. They simply joined whichever club was more convenient. But when I was a youngster it was quite clear that you joined a club according to your politics; or rather, your parents' politics.'

'Wow, what a really weird situation.'

'It seems so now, doesn't it? Maybe, though, you could think of it as something like the racial divisions in America. Think of the times when the society was segregated according to skin color. It's a similar thing, in a way.'

'Well, yes, I guess you're right.'

'The Second World War did a lot to bury the animosities between the two sides,' Päivi went on. 'Reds and whites were fighting on the same side then, against a common enemy, Russia. I think that did a lot to unite the Finnish nation. Or at least, unity grew, like new skin, over the old wounds. The wounds remained under the surface for a long time, but the hostility had mainly disappeared by the fifties and sixties.'

'Well, that was quite a story,' I said, still in a bit of a daze.

'We're a young nation, Len. We've had to cram all our history and growing pains into a relatively short period of time.'

It took some time for this new information to settle in my mind. At first, I kept thinking about the often-heard comment about family history research, that you never know whether you're going to find a murderer among your ancestors. Not that I accepted as a fact that my great uncle Arto was a murderer. Very far from it. But I had certainly come across something wholly unexpected and disturbing. The story of his life and death affected me deeply. It chilled me to the marrow. I had several dreams in the next few nights in which he appeared. Sometimes as a wild and passionate revolutionary; sometimes as a frightened youngster, not much more than a college kid, chased by angry gangs with tracker dogs, hiding in the forest or left bleeding and helpless in the snow. Weird and crazy, as dreams usually are, and all of them bloody.

Chapter Fourteen

Yes, I had been disturbed by Arto's story and I was conscious of being rather subdued in the couple of days immediately following Päivi's revelations. Sufficiently so for her to remark on the change in my spirits. She guessed the cause, too, and started to blame herself for telling it all to me.

'I shouldn't have told you. I'd been avoiding it ever since we started to communicate about your Finnish roots. That was my instinct. I wish now that I'd trusted it.'

'I'd noticed that you never answered my original question about the cause of Arto's death. But I'm glad you told me. I wanted to know the truth. I want to know where I've come from. This is my history and I never knew it before. I'm another link in the same chain of events. I'm the flower that has bloomed on this family tree,' I said with a grin.

Päivi grinned back. 'If you had been a mushroom you would have been a chanterelle, too,' she added, laughing.

'I think that really you *were* obeying your instincts when you told me the facts. You realized that it was the right thing to do because I need to know the truth about my origins.'

This conversation helped to restore my equilibrium a little. Also, I guess I was beginning to come to terms with the facts, and on top of that, I realized that I should make an effort to be more cheerful so that Päivi wouldn't feel that she had caused me to be depressed.

I'd noticed in a tourist information brochure that I'd picked up from the reception desk in my hotel that there was a concert in Lahti that week with Sibelius's violin concerto and the Karelia suite on the program. I thought it would be a great idea to invite Päivi, Marja, Aino and Juho to be my guests at that event. I should certainly listen to Sibelius's music while I was in Finland and I wanted to offer something in return for all the hospitality that I had received. An outing like this would further help to distance the gloom created by Arto's sad history. I made my proposal, suggesting that we could have a meal in Lahti. Päivi reckoned that before the concert would be better than after as Finn's tend to eat early anyway, and dining after the concert would make it very late getting home, what with the drive back as well.

The invitation was passed on to each of them and accepted, and I booked the tickets through the reception at my hotel. The concert started at seven in the evening and it was about an hour's drive to Lahti from Hämeenlinna. We calculated that we should sit down to eat at about five and that we could have an hour and a half to see the center of Lahti. Including the driving time we needed to leave Hämeenlinna at about two thirty.

So we gathered at Päivi's flat on the day of the concert and I was pleased to note an air of positive excitement in our little group. I reckoned that I had hit on a good idea for an outing that everyone would enjoy. We piled into Päivi's car, which was a bit of a squeeze but we managed okay.

When we arrived in Lahti, Päivi parked the car at the harbor and we strolled along the quayside. It was very pleasant beside the lake, with views north towards the open water and some islands. There was a café which was housed in the old railroad station building. Apparently, so Päivi explained, the railroad used to come all the way to the lakeside. That was in the days when the inland waterways were used to transport the logs felled in the central forests. When they arrived at Lahti, they were loaded onto trains to be transported further. Nowadays, it terminated a mile away, on the edge of the town and so the former station building had been converted to this new use.

From the harbor we walked into the center of the town. I have to say that it was not a very inspiring place in terms of architecture and sights. The streets were laid out in a grid design and most of the buildings were modern rectangular blocks. There was little to beguile the eye. The appearance of the town center was similar to Hämeenlinna, in fact; they both looked as if they had been almost entirely rebuilt since the sixties. There are beautiful places outside both towns. Hämeenlinna has a lovely old castle on the outskirts and a park area on the edge of the town which is very scenic and both towns are located beside lakes. But you aren't aware of the water when you're in the town centers, which in both cases kind of struck me as dull and uninteresting.

Lahti, like Hämeenlinna, is not a large town and we had soon wandered as far as a large open space which was the town square. It was quite busy. People were continually passing across it, or standing round in small groups. There were several stalls selling flowers and a stand selling grilled sausages. There was a distinctly holiday atmosphere. We were half way across the square, scanning the surroundings for a likely looking restaurant where we could dine later, when we became aware of some kind of commotion. It was the raised voices that attracted our attention first and then the appearance and body language of the group. Four skinheads were confronting a couple of youngsters who appeared to be of North African origin, by my judgment. The shouting was coming from them, first one then another, making short, barking comments that, although I could understand nothing, were obviously insulting and aggressive. A couple of the skinheads looked barely sixteen, the other two were a bit older, twenty maybe. They seemed to be egging each other on, giving and deriving courage in the manner typical of this kind of group behavior.

128

I was still registering these impressions, which was the mental work of just a second or two, of course, when Aino was already on her way to join the discussion. We hurried after her. As she approached the group she began to address the four skinheads. She didn't raise her voice, nor speak particularly quietly, either. She held eye contact, first with one, then another, round the group. The two younger ones immediately looked rather sheepish, but one of the older skinheads appeared to be a bit more defiant, making replies to what Aino was saying.

I was feeling distinctly nervous myself, as I stood just behind Aino, hoping that I was showing some support and solidarity. I was conscious of how unpredictable these situations can be. You never know how aggressive the actors are, or whether they are armed, high on drugs or simply unbalanced.

Aino was still talking and I felt that the tension had relaxed a bit. I can't explain how I felt it, it was an instinct, but I trusted it and believed that the situation was on the point of dissolving. Three of the four skinheads were moving fractionally back. Juho was beside me and he suddenly reached out, took hold of one of the skinheads' arms and held it. He said something and appeared to be indicating a badge that was sewn onto the sleeve of the boy's olive green bomber jacket. It represented the Finnish flag and had some text beneath that seemed, as far as I could see, to consist of a date. Juho released his arm and the four youths began to move off. There was a last mumbled comment, half thrown over a shoulder and a grunt that might have been an attempt at a sardonic laugh and they were gone.

We looked at each other for a moment.

'Welcome to Finland,' Aino said to the two North African boys.

They smiled shyly. One said, 'Thank you.'

We moved on, in silence at first, and then gradually we relaxed and began to feel more normal. A few minutes later, when we were standing in front of a shop window that Aino and Marja were looking in, I asked Päivi what Aino had been saying and what Juho had meant when he took hold of the boy's arm.

'Oh, Aino basically just gave them a dressing down. Juho was talking about that badge the boy had on his jacket. It showed the Finnish flag with the year of the Winter War against Russia, 1939. There's a lot of pride in the fact that Finland was able to keep the Russian army out of the country at that time and some people may wear the badge to express that feeling, but it has also been adopted as a symbol of nationalism by neo-nazi groups. That's a strong term for kids like those, I know, but I'm afraid ugliness like that can lead all too easily to extremes. Anyway, Juho just said, *I was there*. He's a war veteran from the Winter War, though he never talks about it much.'

'It's often the way, isn't it?' I said.

The incident had left a nasty taste, in my mouth at least. It took me some time to regain my good humor. Aino and Juho very soon appeared to behave as if nothing had happened, strolling about, smiling, looking in the shops. Again, I noticed Juho sometimes watching me with his small, twinkling eyes. The pair of them seemed to have dismissed the incident from their minds as if it was just a case of ignorant kids who needed to be told off by responsible adults. But who knows how the scene would have ended if Aino hadn't intervened? And who knows what Aino and Juho were really thinking? They both had such a calm exterior. However, Päivi was quite right about the dangers of racist attitudes and where they can lead.

We found our restaurant and had a meal, which I have to admit was indifferent at best, but we had a nice time and laughed and told stories, which Päivi translated. The atmosphere was delightful and the food was not so important. We were all back in the right mood again to enjoy the concert by the time we left the restaurant. We strolled back to the harbor area where we'd left the car. The concert hall was right on the lakeside, beside the car park. It was an unusual building which I can best describe as a looking like a huge wooden box placed inside a slightly larger glass case. Picture that, if you can.

Chapter Fifteen

It was well into the second week of my time in Finland and I had passed the half-way point. Three weeks sounds like a longish holiday before it starts, but it's a devilish short time when you're simply living and enjoying life. I'd spent all, or most, of most days with Päivi. We'd very quickly come to feel … What's the right word? … natural? relaxed? at ease? … in each other's company. At least, that's how I felt. I judged that Päivi felt the same. I don't believe I was mistaken about that. We have an instinct that guides us in these cases and it's usually right. But there was rather more to it than that, in my case. It had been very clear to me, ever since that second day at Aino's summer cottage, that I was strongly attracted to Päivi. Nor was this simply the reflex sexuality of noticing a physically attractive woman and responding to her beauty. There are a lot of good-looking women about and, of course, I notice them and register the fact of their attractiveness. That's almost an aesthetic appreciation, in my opinion, and bears no resemblance to the gut-wrenching sensation I felt being close to Päivi.

My instinct didn't help me as to how Päivi felt in this respect. Or maybe I didn't trust it. Or I didn't dare. However, I could not hide the fact from myself, and I wouldn't have wanted to, but it made me very uncomfortable. My second cousin. I tried again to picture what that meant. Our grandfathers had been brothers. One step away from my first cousins in America, who felt almost like brothers and sisters. I didn't like the thought. I didn't like it at all.

But the not liking was all in my mind while my body ached for Päivi. Sometimes I thought that the sooner my stay in Finland was over and I was gone, the better. And then, when we parted at the end of an evening and I returned to my hotel, I couldn't get her out of my mind and passed a restless night and impatient early morning until I could see her again. I felt like a love-sick teenager. I had dreams in which she appeared, often with a content vaguely connected with some event or situation from the day but which would lead, by some weird route, to a touch, a kiss, me holding her in my arms. Sometimes, when I first woke up the next morning, I would be confused as to whether the events in the dream had really taken place the day before and would be half in a panic and half excited until reality kicked back in.

When we had gotten back to Hämeenlinna after our concert trip to Lahti it was only just after ten in the evening. Marja and Juho were both quite tired and wanted to go straight home. Aino was staying the night with Juho and we dropped them off together. That left just Päivi and me and she invited me into her flat for a nightcap. We chatted for about an hour, discussing the music, the performance of the young Russian violinist who had been the soloist, and the architecture of the concert hall. At last I felt it was time for me to be leaving.

As we said goodnight, Päivi gave me a *thank you hug*, as she called it, for such a nice outing. I put my arms round her in response and placed my hands just below her shoulders. I pressed her lightly towards me, conscious of her slim body. Her hair brushed against the backs of my hands. I badly wanted to stroke that hair, stroke the back of her head and neck. I could feel my heart rate accelerate. The memory of her walking into the lake, her bare back, the hair falling over her shoulders and her slim, white behind, came unbidden into my mind. It required a real effort of self-control not to do anything foolish that I would regret horribly the next day. I was quite glad to make my escape, but very restless when I got to my hotel room. I slept badly and woke early.

The next day we had planned to visit the medieval castle of Hämeenlinna. I'd seen it from a distance on several occasions and it was clearly not a place to miss while staying there. It was located just outside the center of the town, on the banks of a channel between two lakes; a strategic location in earlier times and a very picturesque one nowadays.

'You know, Len,' Päivi remarked at one point, as we walked through the building, 'I've sort of gotten the impression that you've lost interest a bit in your family history project. Am I right?'

I smiled. 'Well, yes, I have a bit. It's because I'm having such a great time with the living that I find it less interesting to go looking for the dead. I *am* still interested in the history, of course, but I'd much rather be visiting this castle with you now than going to a municipal office and spending hours going through dreary old records.'

'I thought it was so. But it's not because you think I would be bored, is it? You aren't not doing the research because of me?'

'No,' I answered, smiling. 'Or rather, yes. It's because I'd rather be with you here, or at Aino's cottage, or with you all at the concert in Lahti. All these things we've been doing and the people, family, I'm getting to know; these have become more important to me.'

'That's good then. Would you like to meet some other members of your Finnish family?'

'Of course.'

'Anni and Toni are coming to visit me on Sunday. They'd like to meet you.'

'That sounds great.'

'They can't stay long. They both have summer jobs in Tampere, where they're studying during the term time. But

134

they have Sunday free. I told them they should make the effort to meet you while you're here.'

'I hope you didn't make them feel under an obligation.'

'I guessed you would say that. No, I just reminded them that you were here and wouldn't be staying long. They have their own lives and concerns and they're so active and busy all the time that they forget how quickly the time is passing. They had said from the beginning that they wanted to meet you. They just needed a little reminder. Actually, it was nice for me to have an excuse to urge them to come and visit me. I try not to put pressure on them, usually, but this is a special occasion.'

'How long will they be staying with you?'

'Only a few hours. They won't stay overnight. They'll be out somewhere on Saturday evening and have to be at work early on Monday morning. But they'll probably arrive in time for lunch on Sunday and stay until the early evening. Why don't you come round to my apartment about one o'clock and we'll have lunch and then we'll drive out to Aulanko park and have a walk, if the weather's nice?'

'I'm looking forward to it.'

From the ramparts of the castle we looked across the water towards the same Aulanko park area that Päivi had proposed we might visit on Sunday. From this distance it appeared thickly forested and undulating. It made a beautiful scene, the blue, glittering water, the dark green of the pines and softer green of the birch trees and the pale blue sky and scattered, fluffy clouds. I could have sat and gazed at it for hours.

'Have you been thinking much more about your grandparents and Arto?' Päivi asked gently after a few minutes.

'On and off,' I replied. 'I've wondered how much my own father was affected in his early childhood by those recent memories of his parents. I don't know how much

135

they, his parents, I mean, would have told him about those events. Obviously, not much when he was a small child. It's not a story for little children. And when he was older, I guess they wanted to forget about it. He didn't know about his own father's twin brother until I got the information from you, so he can't ever have heard the facts about Arto, but they might have said something about the civil war in general. Or he might have sensed the painful memories that his parents were carrying in his early childhood. Something in the atmosphere could have been communicated to him. Little kids are like that.'

'Oh, they are,' Päivi agreed.

'Päivi, can I ask you something?'

'Yes, Len, you can ask anything of me.'

'Your father's parents both died when he was very young. Five years old, wasn't he? They died in the same year, when they were only in their thirties. Can I ask how? Was it an accident?'

'No, actually, they both died of pneumonia.'

'It was a big killer in those days. So, what happened to your father? And his brother? Who brought them up?'

'At first both boys stayed with an aunt and uncle on their mother's side. For about a year, if I remember right. Later my father's aunt, Mari, and her husband, Lauri, took my father in and Pentti, my father's brother, went to live with another aunt and uncle, Raisa and Ilpo.'

'Mari was my grandfather's sister, right? And she was Juho's mother, of course.'

'Yes, that's right. My father grew up in their family. Juho was like a big brother to him. That's one reason why I'm very close to Aino and Juho. Plus the fact that they're such lovely people.'

'How sad. His parents dying so young, I mean.'

'Yes, it was very sad. And it left a permanent mark on my father, I believe. His parents had been quite well off.

His father was in business, in construction, and doing well, so I have understood. They had a very nice house in Helsinki, in an area that's nowadays very expensive. I've seen photos of it. It was quite a big house. Everything seemed to be going so well for them. But you can never know, can you? It all fell to pieces.'

'I suppose it was lucky that there were close family who were able to take the boys in and care for them.'

'Yes, of course. But there was a downside to that, too.'

'Oh? How?'

'Well, it comes down to the issue of their property. My father's parents' property. There's some uncertainty about where it went, exactly, and who got what. The one thing that *is* certain is that neither my father, nor his brother, ever inherited anything from their parents.

'There never were any records of what their parents left, or how it was used. The parents died intestate. Under today's laws their property would automatically have been divided between their two sons. One or more legal guardians would have to be appointed nowadays to control the property until the boys were of age. But as far as I know, none of that happened. I don't know what the law required in those days.'

'But wouldn't the money have been used to bring up the boys, pay for their education, whatever?' I asked.

'Of course, there were costs involved in raising the two boys and it was quite reasonable that money from their parents' estate should have been used for that purpose. But no accounts were kept. By the time my father was an adult, those days were already long past. If he had wanted to make enquiries, it would have been difficult to get information, I guess, in addition to being a rather sensitive issue to start investigating.

'I know my father tried to pick up what bits of information he could from general conversation. He spoke

137

to me about it sometimes. Actually, when we went to skiing competitions, when I was still a teenager and could barely understand the issues and concerns myself. He didn't know how much had been raised by selling his parents' house. He didn't know if they had loans or debts. It's probable that they didn't. His father was in the construction business and built the house himself. They weren't extravagant people. The ethic in the Mäkinen family was *Save the money before you buy*. It still was when I was coming to adulthood, but it was especially so back in the twenties and thirties. My father was horrified by the size of the loan Roni and I took to buy our first apartment, which was very modest, I might add. It would have been remarkably out of character for his parents to have had debts or loans.

'Anyway, whatever the sum was, it seems to have been divided mainly between the families that took the boys and nothing more was known about it. It's unlikely that the full sum could have been used on the boys' upbringing.

'And there was the construction business. Presumably it was sold, too, but again there was no record of the transaction or how much money it raised that my father could ever discover. It's possible that some relative or relatives from his mother's family had put money into the business and they wanted to be repaid when it was sold. That's quite reasonable, of course. They may have got back more than they put in. As I said, it was all very unclear.'

'Well, yes, it does sound like quite a muddle.'

'Yeah, it was a muddle. Then there was the furniture, pictures and various household articles from his family home, which was divided between the aunts and uncles. My father told me that he remembered very clearly as a small child going into his relatives' homes and recognizing various items that had come from his own home. In some way, I suppose it was quite natural that the relatives took the furniture since two little boys wouldn't want tables and

138

chairs but even so, it was difficult for my father. As a small child it upset him to see those familiar objects and when he was older and could understand what it meant, it made him quite bitter. Sometimes after we had visited a relative, he would say to me, *I remember that table or carpet, or clock from my parents' home* and I knew he meant more than the words said.

'But then again, I wonder how accurate his memory was. He was only five when his parents died. How could he have remembered so precisely what kind of furniture had been in his childhood home?'

'Hmm, but maybe he wasn't remembering as such,' I suggested. 'In the early days after his parents died, if he visited some relatives he would recognize pieces of furniture by their familiarity. The drastic upheaval in his own life would make those familiar objects all the more significant to him. So later, he would always recognize them, even after the act of remembering had ceased to take place. The knowledge would always already have been there. It originated from a time before his later, adult memory.'

'Yes, maybe you're right. And then, to complicate matters, he felt grateful, genuinely grateful, to the relatives who had taken him and Pentti in. Of course, they were his family, his closest family. He felt more than gratitude; he genuinely liked and loved them. He never fell out with any of his relatives over the issue. In fact, I don't believe he ever actually mentioned it to any of them. Ever. Keep things bottled up inside you was my father's way. But he was always on good terms with all of his relatives. He was always in good spirits at family events and parties. He loved those big family gatherings. He was always popular with everyone and happy to see them. So this kind of secret burden was a constant contradiction for him in his life. Oh, I'm expressing this very clumsily. I'm sorry.'

'No, it's very clear. I understand exactly what you're saying and it sounds very plausible to me.'

'I know he talked to Mom about it because she's mentioned it to me since he died. In fact, she said that there had been some friction between his mother's family and his father's side in the early days. I mean at the time when she and my father were first married. She said that it originated from some disagreement about who had got what from father's parents' estate. I don't know whether father had told her that or whether it was her own idea, though. Like I said, he talked about it to me when I was a kid, and also later, but I don't remember him saying that. He always told me not to talk about it to anyone else. I don't know whether he ever mentioned it to Esko. Probably not. That could have led to repercussions that he wouldn't have wanted. Esko would have been sure to let it out at some time.

'Anyway, it's a long time ago now and it doesn't matter any more, but it mattered to my father. I believe now that it colored his own attitude and behavior when he started his own family. I think that it was very important to him to make a home and have a family to somehow make up for the disruption of his own childhood but at the same time those early experiences made him feel insecure as a husband and father. Ironically, I think he was in a way overcompensating by devoting so much time and energy to me. Ironic, because he was actually making matters worse. It became another source of disappointment to him later. My father died of a heart-attack, but I've always thought that the heart-attack itself was more of a symptom. I think it was disappointment, or a whole series of disappointments, that really killed him.'

'Well,' I said, 'that's another sad story. But what about Aino and Juho? Don't they know anything about what happened inside their family in those days?'

'No. It all happened long before Aino was born. Juho was barely into his teens when my father was taken into their family. I'm sure he would have known nothing about any financial arrangements and probably took no notice of any furniture that might have arrived. In any case, he wouldn't remember now.'

'But maybe you should talk to Aino about it. Just to get it into the open. I don't mean trying to trace any property or anything, but just so that it's not a weight on you, like it was on your father.'

'I have talked to Aino, actually, a few years ago. We had a long heart-to-heart. I made it clear that I wasn't in search of a lost inheritance, that I just wanted to let some light and air into the matter. So she knows at least what my father told me about that time.'

'Well, that's a good thing.'

In silence we watched a small boat for a while glide along the stretch of channel below us, its wake catching the light and spreading out across the water behind it and the sound of its motor floating up to us and then we turned away and went back inside the castle.

Chapter Sixteen

The Sunday when Päivi's son and daughter were visiting started a bit overcast, but by the middle of the morning the sky had cleared and the sun was shining. When I arrived at Päivi's apartment, Anni and Toni were already there and Päivi had decided that instead of eating lunch at home and then going to Aulanko park, it would be nicer to take a picnic and eat it outside as the weather was so pleasant. She was in the middle of getting everything ready. I offered to help, but Anni was already helping in the kitchen, so I sat with Toni and had a chat with him.

Toni was a tall young man. He spoke English fluently and even had an American accent, which he explained by saying that his teacher at upper-secondary school had studied and lived in America for many years. He was very outgoing and confident but without being annoyingly brash or arrogant, as very confident young people can often seem to be. Toni was thoroughly likeable and the longer I talked with him, the more I felt that he was a very well-balanced, straight-forward, open and sincere person. Not so surprising, I added to myself, considering that he was brought up by Päivi.

He talked about his studies and his summer job in a shop in Tampere and asked about my hometown and life in the States. After a while he moved the topic on to politics and was quite diplomatic about asking my opinion on President Clinton's troubles. We discovered that we shared an opinion on that subject. Then we talked about the various things I'd seen and done in Finland. He showed an interest in everything and during that part of the conversation he added a comment that I stored away in my memory to examine more carefully later.

'It's real nice for Mom to have you to show around. It gives her something to do and someone to do it with,' he said, adding, almost as an after-thought, 'she's really quite lonely.'

This was a point of view that hadn't occurred to me at all. Indeed, I had thought that I might be taking up too much of her time and on several occasions I'd expressed that fear to her. She'd always insisted that she was happy to act as my guide and chauffeur, didn't have anything else to do, her friends were working or traveling, and so on. Of course, I believed that was true, but here was another aspect of her life situation to consider which was not necessarily incompatible with her other comments to me. It seemed strange to me to imagine that Päivi could be lonely when she was so lovely. What would she have been doing these days, if I hadn't been here, I wondered.

And then again, what does 'lonely' mean to a twenty-one-year-old? It was in my mind to reply to Toni that his mother would welcome a visit from him more often. I'd registered the slight self-contradiction when she'd denied to me that she'd urged Anni and Toni to visit on my account. However, I guessed that Päivi wouldn't welcome that kind of interference. It wasn't up to me to say anything on the subject. It simply wasn't my business. But I decided that I would try to gauge the extent of Päivi's supposed loneliness, if it existed, because I was troubled by the idea. I didn't at first have any idea how to achieve that, though.

When the picnic was all ready, we set out for Aulanko park. We parked the car beneath an observation tower and walked along a path through the trees that led down to a small lake and continued along the shoreline. We walked for maybe a mile altogether till we came to an area with some wooden benches that each consisted of a length of tree trunk sawn in half lengthways, a table and a place for lighting a campfire. Ready-cut wood was piled under a shelter nearby. The public facilities were certainly well organized, and all of this was free for anyone to come along and use. Toni fetched some of the firewood and started to light a fire. Anni and Päivi unpacked the picnic. They produced several, aluminum foil-wrapped parcels. I didn't know what Päivi had prepared for the picnic lunch and watched these preparations with interest.

'So this one's perch fillets,' Anni said, waving one of the foil parcels. 'In here is new potatoes. And in this one is carrots and fresh coriander. We're going to cook them on open fire. Potatoes and carrots have already boiled enough, so we just have to warm them, and perch fillets are very thin so they will cook fast.'

'It sounds delicious,' I said. 'I thought we'd be having sandwiches.'

'It's the same meal that I'd planned for lunch but we're having it outside,' Päivi said. 'After the main course we'll have melted cheese and cloudberry jam.'

When the fire was ready we laid the foil parcels on the wire mesh and after some fifteen minutes removed and unwrapped them and dished up onto disposable plates. It made a delicious meal, doubly tasty for being prepared and eaten outside. When we'd eaten every last scrap, Päivi produced a blackened coffee pot from a plastic bag and a flask of fresh water, and Toni set about brewing some coffee.

'The Italian prime minister, Berlusconi, was real critical of Finnish cooking in some article I read recently,' Toni said, while we waited for the coffee pot to boil. 'I guess he must have missed grilled perch and Mom's coriander carrots.'

The time passed all too quickly, of course. Before we knew it we were driving Anni and Toni to the railroad station and standing on the platform with them, waiting for their train.

144

'If you guys are ever traveling in the States, you be sure to get in touch,' I told them. 'You'll always be welcome to come and stay and I can show you the sights.'

'Thanks, Len,' they both said.

'Sure. That's what family are for.'

The feeling came over me then that we must have looked like a family in the nuclear sense, standing there on the platform. Päivi and I the parents, seeing off our children. I held on to that fantasy, living it out in my mind, and when Anni and Toni had boarded their train and Päivi and I walked slowly back towards her car, I remarked how quiet it felt when they were gone and there were just the two of us. I guess we were both feeling quite emotional. Päivi put her hand quickly to her eye, as if brushing away a tear. Had she been imagining the same scenario as I had? Or had she been thinking of her ex-husband, wishing that he was there seeing off their children, instead of me? Or was she just saddened by their departure?

As if she'd been reading my mind, Päivi suddenly remarked, 'It's three years ago that Roni and I separated. He lives in Helsinki now. We don't see each other very often. When we do, it's usually to do with something involving Anni and Toni.'

'They're lovely people, your children. You must be very proud of them.'

'I am.'

'Was it a difficult divorce? You don't mind my asking, do you? I thought that as you mentioned the topic, you might want to talk about it.'

'Yes, I think I'd like to talk a bit. To answer your question: yes and no. I suppose all divorces are difficult to some extent, aren't they? Ours wasn't as bad as some others that I've known. And now it's in the past. We can be quite calm around each other.'

'Have you thought of reconciliation?' I asked, wondering if that was the direction the conversation was tending in, and if that was what Päivi wanted to discuss. Not to ask my advice, I don't mean. I couldn't advise. But merely to clarify her own thoughts. I recalled the exclamation mark that she'd placed in the email after the reference to reverting to her maiden name when she first mentioned her divorce in an email more than a year earlier. It might have been indicative of pain and loss, or then again, of resentment; whatever. I very much wanted to know.

'Heavens, no.'

She was quite emphatic. So that wasn't it.

'I guess that three years is time enough to get over the worst,' I ventured, picking up an earlier thread.

'Oh yes, it is.'

'May I ask if there's a new man in your life?'

I didn't like the sound of the question much, it felt a bit like prying, and the phrasing sounded priggish. Why are some topics so damned difficult to talk naturally about? But Päivi had embarked on the subject herself and had said she wanted to talk about it. That seemed to give me excuse enough. To be honest, I was pretty sure there couldn't be any serious relationship or I would surely have met the man by now, unless he was away for some reason, in which case, Päivi would almost certainly have mentioned him. However, I won't make any secret of the fact that I was curious to hear what Päivi would say on the subject, both for my own reasons and because I was thinking about Toni's remark that his mom was lonely.

'No,' she replied. 'I went out a few times with a girlfriend who'd also been recently divorced. We both wanted to meet another man. We were quite open about that with each other and we wanted to have some moral support, so we had a few nights out. I hated it. Sitting in bars, or going to awful dancing places. We even went to a nightclub

146

where most people were about Anni's and Toni's age. Oh well, those places aren't so awful, I suppose, if you like them and want to be in them. I didn't. I felt thoroughly out of place. Probably I was being over-sensitive but I didn't enjoy it. I stopped going after a few times. It was about a year or so ago.'

'It must be difficult,' I said, trying to put sympathy into my voice.

'I'm sorry, Len, burdening you with my troubles like this.'

I reached out and took hold of one of her hands.

'Not at all,' I said. 'I just wish there was something more that I could do.'

'You do plenty by just being here and listening. You're a very good listener, Len, and it's easy to talk to you.'

I had kept hold of her hand and now drew it under my arm. I placed my other hand over hers and gave it a slight squeeze.

'Let's walk a little way,' I suggested. And so we set off, arm in arm, just as if we had been a couple for many years, I thought.

Chapter Seventeen

It was a couple of days after this conversation, with the end of my visit clearly in sight, that Päivi told me she'd had a phone call from Juho, who was keen to see me. At first, I understood that she meant he would like to see me before I left Finland, and I said that of course I wouldn't leave without saying goodbye. That wasn't it, though.

'He said that he'd found some more letters from your grandfather and that he wants you to know what's in them.'

It sounded intriguing. It also sounded a bit ominous. Ever since learning about Arto, I'd come to associate my grandparents' departure from Finland in 1920 with tragedy. Was there going to be some further twist?

'Do you know what kind of information they contain?' I asked.

'No. Juho didn't say.'

I remembered how I'd noticed the way that Juho sometimes watched me, as if he was thinking about something. It occurred to me now that maybe he'd known about these letters all the time and had been trying to decide whether to tell me whatever it was that they contained, or keep it hidden.

'When should we go to see him?'

'We could go now, if you want.'

'Let's. I'm burning with curiosity.'

When we arrived at Juho's apartment, he seemed to have been expecting us, or at least was prepared for our arrival; on his table was an ancient-looking wooden box, something like an old drawer, that was filled with yellowed and foxed papers. Before he showed us any letter, though, we went to his kitchen where he made a pot of coffee and put a plate of biscuits ready. These preparations complete, we returned to the living room and sat round the table. The coffee was poured, the plate of biscuits handed round, and then Juho extracted a letter from the box. He handed it to Päivi with a comment in Finnish and seemed to be indicating some passages. I waited while Päivi ran her eye down the page, turned to the next page and read on in silence. At last she turned back to the first sheet and made them tidy.

'Shall I translate this to you?' she asked.

'Please.'

'It begins with the usual greetings and reports about health. I'll skip that. Then it goes on:

'*We are now living in Duluth where we have rented a small but clean apartment and I have work in a mill. The pay is quite good and I am satisfied. Sylvi has the chance of some domestic work, too, so we have enough and can even save some money.*

'*There are a lot of Finnish families here and we stick close together. People are ready to help each other, which is good.*

'*And now I must come to some bad news. It looks like the community here in Duluth is unsettled and violent. Two days ago there was a riot in the town. A very large crowd of the local population gathered in the streets. They were very angry and shouting all the time. I didn't understand everything at the time because I don't know the language so well yet. Some Finnish friends have explained that the mob, who were all white people, were angry against the colored people. They said that a white woman had been raped by black men and this is why they wanted to punish the black men. But they didn't get the men who raped the woman, they got three other men who were colored and hanged them in the street …*'

'A lynching! In Duluth? Jesus Christ, I've never heard about that. It's horrible.'

'*….They didn't care if they were the guilty men or not, they just wanted to kill colored men. It is like in Finland in the war when reds and whites killed each other. We don't know what this means but we are very worried that there may be more fighting and killing. We hope not.*'

149

I was speechless for a while. I was remembering my grandparents as I had known them, and then trying to picture them witnessing a lynching. The two images just wouldn't sit side-by-side in my imagination. It was impossible for me to understand that the grandparents I had known had had an experience like that locked in their memories.

'It must have been a shock for them, arriving in an unknown country, to come up against that kind of situation,' I said at last. 'They must have been terrified.'

'Awful. And it reminded them of the killing in our civil war, too.'

Juho handed Päivi another paper from the box and said something softly.

'There's another letter,' Päivi said. 'Shall I read it as well?'

'Yes, please.'

'This time there's almost no preamble. Your grandfather writes:

'*You remember I told you about the riot and the murder of the three men in the street in my last letter. Now we have learned about another very bad thing. Many Finns are talking about it because of what has happened here.*

'*Two years ago, one of us, a Finn, was killed by a mob. They broke into his home and dragged him out and carried him away. No one knew what had happened to him for a few days but then his body was found in the forest. He had been hanged, like the other men. They say he was tarred and feathered, too.*

'*I heard this from other Finns who have been here longer. They remember the man, his name was Olli Kinkkonen. He was from Ostrobothnia. They said that the mob was angry because Finnish workmen had made a union and demanded more salary. When the employer didn't give it, they organized a strike. This made the local people very angry. They don't like unions, or for working men to go on strike. They said that we Finns are communists and trouble-makers because we have unions.*

'*The mob murdered this Olli Kinkkonen because he was a Finn, not because he was a striker. The ones who remembered him say he was never in a strike. They say that we Finns have to be careful in the town. There are some places where it is better not to go. Especially now, when the atmosphere is bad and tense. I don't understand too well how bad it is. I hope the local people aren't angry that we have come here to work. I think there are plenty of jobs but some people maybe don't like us coming here. We will be very careful and not go out much after dark. The Finnish families stick together. That is a good thing.*'

'Well, that's all news to me. I've never heard anything about this kind of unrest and murder in Duluth. Duluth, of all places. It's so middle-class and decent. It's a bad business.'

'It's a long time ago now. People forget.'

'Maybe. I suppose so. I bet my grandparents didn't forget.'

'No, not the people who experienced it at first hand, perhaps. There can't be many people alive now who remember it, though. And those who might remember would have been children at the time.'

I was deeply disturbed by the events described in my grandfather's letter and it took a bit of time for me to assimilate it all, but gradually I began to understand better what it must have really felt like for them to find themselves in the middle of such hatred in a strange country, knowing the language imperfectly. And on top of everything else, having just left a civil war behind them that had cost the life of my grandfather's brother. These thoughts were colored by the general sense of horror at the deaths of the three black men and Olli Kinkkonen.

'Juho says that he thought you should know about these facts because it's important to know the truth about history, but he hopes you aren't offended that he showed you these letters,' Päivi explained, after Juho had spoken to her in a little above a whisper.

'Offended?' I repeated, rather surprised.

'That's the word he used. I think he means that you might feel it's a slur against your own countrymen that they did these things. There is, or rather there used to be, that kind of sensitivity in Finland about the events of the civil war.'

'He thinks of me as an American. Well, yes, of course, I am. But I'm not offended. No, not at all. I have only horror and abhorrence of that lynching mob mentality. I think that it should always be recognized and opposed, especially in one's own nation. I hope I would have the courage to oppose it, if it was ever necessary. Juho is right. It's important to know the truth about history.'

Päivi passed my comments on to Juho who stood up and solemnly shook my hand.

We left Juho's apartment and made our way into the center of the town. By this stage my mind and thoughts were filled with images of the lynchings, the baying of the mob, the fear of the victims, the fear, probably, of half the individuals in the mob of seeming to be half-hearted, which very possibly made them the most active. What a mess human psychology is. These images somehow got mixed up with the execution of Arto, my imagination producing pictures from these tragedies at random.

'Are you feeling okay, Len?' Päivi asked, breaking in on my thoughts.

'Sorry,' I replied, 'I've been a bit self-absorbed, haven't I? Just thinking.'

'Why don't you come to my apartment for dinner this evening?'

'Thanks, that would be lovely. And why don't we stop at this bar now and have a little aperitif?' I added, indicating an establishment that we were just passing. 'And then we can go to the liquor store and I'll get a nice bottle of wine to have with the meal.'

By nine o'clock that evening we'd eaten well and were feeling the effects of the alcohol we'd consumed. The topic of the letters and the lynchings and what it had meant to my grandparents had come up repeatedly throughout the evening. Each time we dropped it, ten minutes later, we were talking about it again.

'I'm so amazed that I'd never heard about this before. I've lived all my life in Minnesota. Duluth is virtually just down the road. Okay, there aren't many people now who remember those events, but when I was twenty there were plenty. Well, obviously no one talked about it.'

Later I became more emotional.

'God dammit. Those people,' I ranted, thinking of the entire Finnish-American community, 'traveled half way round the world to get away from war and killing and terror. Peaceful people who just wanted a job and a life and to be paid – God dammit – a pittance, when all's said and done, for their labor. And they find themselves in the same kind of shit, damn situation that they thought they'd left behind. God dammit. My grandfather's twin brother murdered, and he wanted to leave it all behind and found himself in a damned lynching community. The smug murdering bastards. God dammit. And my own father born into that fear and not even understanding why he was afraid. And still is. God dammit.'

'Len.'

'God dammit.'

'Yes, you've said that, Len. Calm down now.'

Päivi put her arm around my shoulders. I realized with some surprise that I had tears in my eyes.

'I'm sorry,' I said. 'I guess I got carried away.'

'Don't think about it any more today.'

I was over-wrought. I could feel my heart pumping. Päivi rubbed my shoulders. I turned my head and looked towards her. She patted my back and I squeezed her other hand, as I had done the evening that we took Anni and Toni to the station. She was all sympathy, and although I might easily have begun to feel foolish about my outburst, her sympathy soothed me. And so she comforted me.

Chapter Eighteen

I don't know why I got so worked up and upset that evening. It was a nasty story, of course, but it didn't touch me personally and, looking back, my reaction seems out of all proportion. I guess the truth is that it was not only about the events in Duluth in 1920. I was already in an emotional state, what with my feelings about Päivi and my discomfort with them, the knowledge that I would soon be leaving Finland and my new-found family and all that it, and they, had meant to me. I'd started to feel as if I had always lived there and belonged. Then I was stressed about returning to my old life in America when I felt so changed, almost a different person. And, although I hadn't recognized it at that time, I was stressed about returning to Helen. All these emotions were at work inside me, waiting for some kind of release, and the information contained in my grandfather's letters was the trigger that set me off.

The last few days of my time in Finland flew by and, before I knew it, I was saying my farewells to Aino and Juho and Marja. On my last evening we all collected at Päivi's apartment.

'We've bought you a goodbye present,' Päivi said and she produced three books. 'It's an English translation of a novel called *Under the North Star* by Väinö Linna. It's a trilogy,' she explained. 'The story and characters continue from volume to volume, but each volume is also a complete novel on its own. It's one of the greatest works of Finnish literature and it will tell you a lot about the history and birth of the Finnish nation and also about the civil war. That comes in volume two. You will understand us better after reading it.'

'Thank you all very much. That's a wonderful gift. I shall read it many times and always think of all of you as I do.'

I handed round the gifts that I had bought for them. We tried to be merry but the atmosphere was inevitably a bit subdued.

'You must all come to the States sometime,' I told them. 'You'll always find a bed and a warm welcome in Minnesota. I'd love to see you there and show you round. I'd like to be able to return some of the wonderful hospitality I've met with here in Finland.'

My invitation was gratefully received, but I can't say it was exactly pounced on. Aino said, 'Yes, maybe, one day.' Juho smiled and said nothing. Marja, so Päivi translated, said that she wasn't sure how to get there.

'And what about you?' I said to Päivi. 'Do you think you would one day come to visit me in Minnesota?'

'I don't know, Len. I'd like to, of course. I'll think about it. Maybe one day.'

'Well, I want you to know that it's a serious invitation and it's always open.'

'Can I teach you my favorite Finnish word, Len?' Päivi said a little bit later.

'Sure,' I replied.

'It's *suvaitsevaisuus*. I love it because it sounds so musical.'

She said it again and I tried to repeat it. After several attempts I managed something approaching the sound when Päivi said it.

'What does it mean?' I asked.

'Tolerance.'

'From now on, that's an idea that I will always associate with you, then.'

'It has a lovely, lilting rhythm. It's like poetry.'

'Yes, I think I know what you mean.'

'Do you like poetry, Len?'

'I don't read very much of it, I'm afraid.'

'I read a lot. I love it. I write poetry, too. Maybe I'll try to write some in English one day.'

156

'I hope you'll send them to me, if you do.'

The next day I was traveling to Helsinki. My flight back to the States, via London, left Helsinki very early in the morning and I'd decided to stay the night before in Helsinki so that I wouldn't need to travel there the same morning. We said our final farewells on Hämeenlinna railroad station platform. There were one or two tears which were quickly wiped away and we tried to look bright and cheerful. I hate goodbyes. In a way I was thankful to be on the train and moving, but I felt dreadfully empty.

In Helsinki I checked into my hotel and went up to my room. I felt restless and started to wander around the corridors quite aimlessly. In this way I came across the hotel sauna. There was a sauna time early in the morning which was long over now. I tried the door, expecting it to be locked but it opened. I went inside. It was dark but I found a light switch and turned on the light in the dressing room. I went through to the door to the hot room and went inside. The sauna stove was electric, of course, and it was turned off but there was still some warmth left from the morning session. The thermometer on the wall read between 35 and 40 degrees centigrade which I estimated to be somewhere around 90 degrees Fahrenheit. It was quite dark in the hot room after I had closed the door. I stood there in the warm darkness. It felt like being in the womb, I thought. I closed my eyes and focused my attention on the feeling of warmth. I imagined going to sleep in there. I fancied myself lying on the shelf beside a warm stove in an old house in the country during winter.

'Pankkouuni,' I said aloud to myself.

Chapter Nineteen

I arrived back home. It felt very strange. For a few days I felt a bit depressed. I was a different person in some ways, but I was also still the same old Len Makinen. Helen had enjoyed her summer holiday in the States. She'd spent a lot of time visiting her relations. So, much the same as me, in fact. She even showed some interest in what I had done and what I'd seen. The time apart had maybe been good for us. I gave a showing of my photographs from the trip to Helen, the boys and a couple of neighbors one evening, and it was a great success.

I joined a local Finnish society and I gave a talk and slide show there about my trip to Finland and my family roots. I kept the family history part to a minimum, partly out of necessity since I didn't actually have an awful lot of information to tell, but also because I reckoned that most of my audience would have had a limited interest in my family past. But what I did – and I'm rather proud of the way I structured it – was to use my family history research trip as a framework for talking about Finnish history, landscape and geology, art, culture and traditions. I talked about the Finnish civil war of 1918 and my great uncle Arto's part in it and his death. I described my grandparents' arrival in America and their experiences in Duluth. There were some wet eyes in that part of my talk.

I even joined a class in Finnish language, run by the Finnish society, despite what I'd said to Taru. I felt a twinge of conscience about that, actually. I'd been unnecessarily dismissive of her offer of help and now I might have benefitted from it. I realised that I wasn't myself as tolerant as Päivi and the Finnish Mäkinens.

So I began to get assimilated, or I assimilated myself, back into the old way of life. But with this difference: I had been into that empty area in what had made me what I am. I guess I could say I had filled out as a person. I felt so, at least.

Very soon after my return to the States, I tried to find out more information about the events in Duluth in 1918 and 1920. In the year 2000 it wasn't easy to get hold of facts, but I did discover that a book had been written by Michael Fedo in 1977 about the lynchings. The author had tried to raise public awareness about what had happened, but at the time the book had created little impact and was soon forgotten.

I managed to get hold of an old copy and so learned more about the events. It was clear that the white Anglo-Saxon community had been in denial about the affair for decades and certainly didn't welcome Michael Fedo's attempts to open up the matter. However, by a coincidence, just around the same time that I was trying to find out about these events, that attitude was changing. There was a growing movement in Duluth itself to acknowledge the facts of history by some public action. A committee was formed to consider the best way that this might be done. Nowadays, a memorial to Isaac McGhie, Elmer Jackson and Elias Clayton stands in downtown Duluth on the street corner where the three men were murdered. A memorial to Olli Kinkkonen has been set up on his grave by the Finnish community.

After decades of erasure, the truth is now public. Everyone, including readers of my story, can check out the facts on the website of Minnesota Public Radio where there's a series of articles about the lynching of the three men and a further article about the Finn.

No one who remembers the events first hand is alive today, of course, but the articles contain material from interviews that were recorded some thirty or forty years ago. I was struck, and deeply affected, by this comment from the second article, titled, 'The memories fade, except among the blacks', written by Chris Julin and Stephanie Hemphill:

> *Newspapers fell silent about the lynching. It didn't make the history books. But black people in Duluth never stopped telling the story – quietly – after church, or over the kitchen table.*

So, while the whites were practicing communal amnesia, the black community preserved the memory to serve as a warning of what had happened and could happen again. For some time, at least, the knowledge would surely have been kept alive in the tight-knit Finnish community also, for the same reason.

The article about the murder of Olli Kinkkonen, titled, 'The other lynching in Duluth', by Chris Julin, includes part of an interview with Donald Wirtanen, a former honorary Finnish consul in Duluth, who was five years old in 1918 and who remembered his parents talking about the case and remembered, also, the horror of the disrespect the murderers showed for their victim:

> *Here was a Finnish man who was tarred and feathered. That was terrible news for a five-year-old,' recalls Wirtanen. 'And then of course, there was much more said about this in 1920 because of the lynching of the three young black men here.*

My grandparents arrived in the middle of these events and my father was born just two years later into this atmosphere. At that time the stories would still have been fresh in the minds of the black and Finnish communities. As a small child he must have felt this atmosphere without understanding it, probably without hearing all the facts at a very early age. By the time he was older, and might have been given such information, the family had left Duluth. With the passage of several years, perhaps the Finns, unlike the black community, allowed the events to sink into oblivion. In any case, I am sure that my father knew nothing of the facts but I believe that he carried the burden of submerged knowledge with him.

For me, the discovery of all this cast a new light on my father's attitude and behavior. I'd always explained his attitude to his Finnish heritage as his making a choice between being a Finn or being an American. I'm sure that that was part of it, but I now understood that there must also have been far deeper and more serious motives at work which made him feel that it could be unsafe not to advertise, in a way, his commitment to America. This has made me extremely suspicious of any pressure placed on individuals to make any kind of choice between the country they live in and the country where their family roots are. I can see neither any need nor justification for that.

Chapter Twenty

The years have rolled by. It's five years ago that I travelled to Finland. Päivi has not visited Minnesota. She hasn't indicated that she is likely to come in the near future either, but more than a year after I returned from Finland, she sent me some poems about some of the events that she had related to me and which I've recounted in this Finn's tale. In the email that the poems were attached to, she pointed out that in the poems she'd made some changes to the actual facts because she felt that the adjustment suited the poems.

One of the most important alterations to reality, she wrote, was changing her sport from skiing to swimming for the contrast that offered with the near-drowning of her toddler brother. She'd also made the scene of the near-drowning the lagoon, whereas it was actually by some rocks on the outer shore of the island, though she said that she doesn't know the exact spot where it happened. The brother in the poems is younger than the narrator, who represents herself. She explained that as she imagined these scenes so intensely she felt herself to be actually present and that it felt right and logical to represent herself as aware, in the poems, of the events as they took place and that meant she needed to be older than she really was. I guess it's okay to change reality in a poem, that's why it's called fiction. We sure as hell can't change the past in reality, though we can learn to see and understand that past differently and that can change the way we feel ourselves to be.

I know that from my own experiences and maybe it's happening inside us all the time, subconsciously, often in small ways that accumulate and change the idea we have of what has formed us, and therefore of what we are.

However, I'm not a literary person, and these ideas are a bit deep for me, but I reckon the poems look pretty good and so I've included them here. Päivi added an epigraph to the poems, 'These be the verses'. I don't know the significance of that and I didn't ask as I have the idea that you shouldn't ask a poet what their poems mean and I guess the same applies to the epigraph.

-oOo-

These be the verses.

Fire

I lit a candle of remembrance
for what was lost and gone.
The flame clung to the wick
and fattened. Wax melted,
transforming itself.
I tended the flame,
grew warmer in the process.
I dipped a pen in my sweat
and started to write.

Kelvenne

Yesterday I visited the lagoon
where we spent our childhood summers.
Its steep, gloomy shore dropped
into tar-colored water.
I think the lagoon is older than the lake.
It's the seed that
the lake has grown from.

There was never a ripple
to disturb the surface
unless we made it.
The reeds on the sandbank that barred
the entrance swayed in the wind
and the rustle floated across
the still lagoon like a whisper.

You were never afraid
of the monster that watched us
from the black-brown depths.
When I ran back to the sun
you climbed branches that overhung
the water that had overwhelmed you.

Did you remember that day
when *tick-tock* was the beat of your heart
as the seconds passed
with your face in the water?
No one knows how long you floated,
your arms and legs drifting wide,
little two-year-old star.

Yet the lagoon held no fear for you.
I wonder, was the lack in you always,
or was that its beginning?

Star Gazing

There's something in my eye
like the dead cells that float
across the field of vision.
Blink, and they jump,
hesitate, then drift on.

Moonlit midnight. The lagoon
is a bright eye in a dark socket,
watching upward.
The lake is composed of all the tears it has cried.
I lie at the bottom of the lagoon
on the ancient, magic sand,
see with its eye, the fish swim past,
boats and clouds glide overhead,
the stars move across the sky.

There's something in my eye,
shaped like a star that floats
like a dead cell across my field of vision.

To My Brother

You were always the one who got
to stay at home. I, the one
who got taken to stay with relatives,
made a fuss over, the champion swimmer.

Training occupied my time
and father's: driving me to the pool
or competitions, counting and timing
my lengths, totting up the miles,
supervising my diet.
Even Mom became jealous.

I was daddy's girl and his pride.
When I won, I could feel how he glowed.
My swimming became the denial
of your accident.

You were always the one who got
left behind, and though you were fast
you could only career into the barriers,
never jump over them. Unable to sit still
or concentrate, you were never able to get clear.

Was it all in your genes? Or was it
the damage done by near-drowning?
Or perhaps it became your protest
at being always the one who never got there,
no matter how fast you rushed.

To My Mother

As a young mother with toddlers,
tied to the house in a tedious village
through months of grey days, snow and rain,
I can imagine how much you enjoyed
the summer escape to the lakeside –
light and the constant activity and company.

I can picture my brother and me
on the beach, scrambling on rocks.
I can believe him the more daring,
edging further, over dark water.
I can understand that a mother's
attention is momentarily distracted
till the absence of children's voices
calls it back.

I can empathize with panic,
the twist in the gut and horror
of a child floating face down and still.

I can sympathize with the reaction,
composed of relief and guilt, that leads you
decades later to retell it
as a humorous anecdote: He lived,
therefore it turned out all right.

I can believe his erratic behavior,
inability to concentrate, his early
death, all derived from lack of oxygen
to his brain. All these I can;
but I cannot tell you what I think.

To My Father

The peat's surface showed no sign
but deep in its heart
the peat bog smoldered,
intense heat creeping ever deeper
and spreading wider.

Winter snow and the spring melt
couldn't deaden the bog fire.
Rain and storms came and went.
The bog fire outlasted
the seasons and the years.

There came a day in autumn
when the air looked hazy,
odor of charred wood on the wind
that stung my eyes
until they watered.

To Roni

From the start I pursued ideal visions,
took familiar prejudices

and the words of pop songs seriously.
I see myself now as a flame

that flickered and beat wings of fire
to escape from a waxen image.

Lost in my own thoughts,
how could I have known what you were thinking?

A Moment Shared With Len In Finland

Then we came into the valley where curling ferns grow
thigh high, pushing their tendrils from spongy soil.
You drank at the spring where the pearly runnel flows
from the fecund earth's dark core to uncoil
and snake over water-darkened moss.
You pressed your mouth into the narrow cleft,
breathed in its dank and secret scent
while I stood over you and watched
you quench your thirst, then knelt –
oh, a little ungainly – and happily satisfied mine.

To Len

I hope you found what you came
half way round the world in search of.
I know I little expected
what you were bringing to me
as I waited for your train to arrive.

As a child, I pictured the preface
to each new meeting
as a predestined progress,
inevitably drawing two people together.

History delivered you to me.
I hope you know what you took with you when you left.

-oOo-

Oh, Päivi.

About the Author

Mike Horwood has lived in Finland since 1985. He studied for an MA in creative writing at Manchester Metropolitan University and is currently working towards a PhD at Bangor University. He has published a translation from the Finnish of Martti Hynynen's collection *island, nameless rock* with Cinnamon Press, and many of his poems have appeared in magazines and anthologies. Ward Wood has also published his poetry collection *Midas Touch*.

Acknowledgements

My thanks to Adele Ward for her clear-sighted editing work on this novel and to Mike Fortune-Wood for another striking cover design.

Special thanks to Shauna Busto for reading the manuscript and making many useful suggestions.

I am grateful to Minnesota Public Radio for permission to reproduce material from their website.

Excerpt from:
'The memories fade, except among the blacks'
by Chris Julin and Stephanie Hemphill
(c)(p) 2001 Minnesota Public Radio.
Used with permission. All rights reserved.

Excerpt from:
'The other lynching in Duluth' by Chris Julin
(c)(p) 2001 Minnesota Public Radio.
Used with permission. All rights reserved.

Excerpts available at:
http://news.minnesota.publicradio.org/projects/2001/0
6/lynching/